THE THIEF BEFORE CHRISTMAS

Counterfeit Capers

SLOANE STEELE

Chapter One

*L*ondon George sat on the floor of her studio, surrounded by paintings that were not hers. Well, she'd painted them, but they were not her concepts, her visions. They were all forgeries.

Damn good ones at that.

But she was in a rut. She hadn't been inspired to create anything of her own for too long. Maybe she'd lost her artistic mojo.

She flopped back on the floor and stared at the ceiling. From her position, she could see out one of the high windows on the opposite wall of her loft. She hadn't been outside all day, but she knew it was chilly. Fall barely blinked by and winter was heading in. Suddenly, she knew what she needed to do: decorate for Christmas.

She jumped up from the floor and went to her everything closet. She called it that because she put everything in there that she didn't know what to do with. After shoving a few boxes out of the way, she found the bin she was looking for.

She dragged it out to the middle of the room and removed the lid.

The state of the lights left her disappointed in past London. When was going to learn to be more patient and put the light away without jumbling them? She pulled out the clump of lights and sat on the couch to detangle them. Once she had the first string free, she climbed on a chair and began hanging them.

They were sloppily dangling, but she didn't care. She plugged in the one lonely string so she could feel some progress. As soon as the twinkling colorful bulbs lit up, she felt happier.

Christmas had always been her favorite time of the year—when she was little, before her parents made a bunch of money and began traveling the world.

She was halfway through detangling the second string when her doorbell rang. She dropped the lights, surprised, because she wasn't expecting anyone.

Sliding open the heavy metal door to the loft, she was greeted by a strange quiet. Normally, the co-op space was extremely noisy, from metal bands practicing to metal sculptors banging away. Today, silence.

She opened the front door, and Nikki stumbled in, handing her an empty bottle of wine.

"Hi. How are things?" she asked, seeing that Nikki was already buzzed.

"Good, I guess. I've been a little restless with nothing to do." She strode into London's loft and went straight to grab another bottle of wine. She filled their usual mismatched coffee cups.

"Shocker." Nikki didn't do well with time off. And their heist crew was on a bit of a hiatus to let things cool off.

"Whatever. Audrey said to meet her here." Nikki plopped on the couch.

"Okay." She waited a minute, but Nikki gave her nothing else. "How's Wade?"

"A pushy ass."

London snickered. Now, she was getting somewhere. Her boyfriend did something to piss her off. She sat down beside Nikki.

"I mentioned that Audrey and Jared were working through the list of art trying to figure out who's insured by someone other than Atlas so we could go after them. He suggested we run a con to get better access to these guys and the art. An inside man."

It made sense. Didn't explain why it would irritate Nikki. "Doesn't Jared count as our inside man?" London asked, referring to Audrey's boyfriend, who also bankrolled their operation.

"Jared isn't Mia. As much as she annoyed me, she had a knack for knowing what to look for."

London patted her thigh. "I miss her, too. Why is this a problem?"

"Because Wade is trying to get involved. Be *helpful*." Nikki sneered as she put air quotes around *helpful*.

"He is a good con man. What's the issue?"

Nikki gulped her wine and refilled her cup. "Wade is clean. He got out of this life. I don't want to be the cause of his downfall. Backsliding into a life of crime."

"So you're what? Trying to save him? Protect him from himself?"

Nikki glared.

London sipped her wine and went back to detangling her lights. "Not to be a bitch in pointing this out, but have you considered how well that kind of attitude has worked in this little group of ours? Jared tried to protect Audrey. Wade tried to protect you. Neither handled it very well."

"Not to be a bitch, but what the hell are you doing?" Nikki asked, pointing at the lights.

London smiled. "Hanging my Christmas decorations."

"It's November."

"I know!"

"Oh, God. You're one of those, aren't you? I should've guessed. All excited for a holiday."

"You know it."

"I'm gonna need more wine." She refilled her cup again.

"Wade's a big boy. He can make his own decisions," London said, going back to their conversation as she handled the mangled string of lights.

"He has more at stake now. We're not kids with nothing. He has a life and a business."

"So tell him we don't need help. We'll back you up."

Nikki groaned. "But I'm selfish. I *want* to work with him. Stealing the Devereaux from the Carlisle Museum was fun. Watching him teach Mia to run a con? Hilarious. I hadn't realized how much I missed working with him." She glugged down more wine.

The doorbell rang again and London went to let Audrey in.

"Hey," Audrey said. "Did you get my message?"

"No. I must've forgotten to charge my phone. But Nikki's here."

"Good." As they walked down the hall toward the loft, Audrey pulled off the kit beanie she often wore and shook out her dark brown hair.

"Eh. You might want to reserve that judgment until you see her."

"Oh, no. What happened?"

"She's fighting with Wade."

"Am not," Nikki yelled from inside the loft.

After closing the door behind them, London said, "So what's up? Did you and Jared figure out how to move forward?"

"Pshh," Nikki waved a hand as she filled her mug again. She pointed at Audrey. "No offense to your boyfriend, but we'd've been fine without the major pause."

Audrey sighed. "He wouldn't have made us stop without reason. There was too much suspicion."

"What's the plan? It'd be great to get rid of some of these." She gestured to the canvases in the corner of the room. Then, she scooped up the tangled lights and shoved them on top of the bin so Audrey could sit.

"What's with the lights?" Audrey asked. "A little early, isn't it?"

"I was bored and feeling sad. Christmas makes me happy."

"Okay," Audrey continued, "Jared and I have

been poring over the notes Mia left us about the art and the owners. So far, we've only found five pieces that are insured by a company other than Atlas."

She handed London a piece of paper.

Before looking at it, London asked, "I'm still not sure what the big deal is about taking the ones Atlas insures. We're not taking from Atlas."

"Atlas is scrutinizing everything right now because of the rash of forgeries provided by us. If they think it's an inside job, they might start re-evaluating all the pieces they insure. If they authenticate one on the list that we haven't gotten to, they'll pay out when we do get to it."

London nodded. "I guess that does ruin the whole revenge-embarrassment plan. Okay, so we move on to other pieces and give Atlas a reprieve."

"Plus, Atlas is the only link the FBI has."

She unfolded the paper and looked at the list.

"Maybe some of what you have here is ready to go?" Audrey asked hopefully.

London sighed. "Only one. It's a small one, but the Leach painting is ready. I haven't even started on the rest of these."

The last item on the list caught her eye. She waved the paper at Audrey. "What is this? A tree topper?"

Audrey didn't take the sheet. Didn't even look at it. Instead, she looked at London as if she was stupid. "It's the thing that goes on top of a Christmas tree."

London closed her eyes for a moment. "I know what a tree topper is. How is this art?"

"Oh. It's hand-blown glass encrusted in diamonds." Audrey set her mug on the table and pulled out her phone. A few swipes and she turned the screen to London.

London took the phone and zoomed in. "We have a problem. I don't know how to do glass. I've never worked in glass as a medium. Unless I smashed it to make a mosaic."

Audrey blew out a breath. "I was afraid of that, and I did some digging. I thought I had a solution. One of the victims on our list was actually a glassblower."

"No way."

"Yeah. I figured two birds, one stone, you know? Call them up, commission the tree topper and pay them an exorbitant amount of money for it. Then we get a forgery and take their name off the list."

"But?" London asked hesitantly.

"The dude's shop closed down. His son has his own shop, so I called him. When I asked about a specific custom piece, he shut me down flat. Wouldn't discuss it and practically hung up on me."

"Damn. Should've known it wouldn't be that easy. I still don't know how to blow glass."

"Well, babe," Nikki said, slapping London's thigh, "it's a good thing you have a month to learn."

A month? To learn how to blow glass and come up with reasonable fake diamonds? "Why a month? It's not even Thanksgiving. Plus, most people leave the tree up until the new year."

Nikki laughed. It was not a good sound. It

held just enough of an edge that London knew there were more problems besides the fact that she didn't know how to blow glass.

Audrey reached for the wine bottle and topped off London's cup. "The tree topper belongs to Bruce Moore. He has an annual Christmas party. Huge bash. His Christmas trees are legendary."

"And?"

"The tree is up for exactly one week. He always has a real tree delivered and decorated the weekend before the party. The day after the party, the tree is taken down and all decorations put back in storage because he spends the rest of the holiday season in Barbados." Nikki leaned back and spread her arm along the back of the couch.

"Wow." London had nothing else to say to that. "That's..."

"Ridiculous?" Audrey offered. "Not worth our time?"

London turned to the hacker. "If it's not worth our time, why do it? Why not skip this one?"

"Because it's a challenge," Nikki said with a gleam in her eye. "We have plenty of time to case the house and watch the staff. A week is plenty of time to break in. And worthwhile? It's covered in fucking diamonds. It's worth more than some of these masterpieces we've been dealing with."

"I wanted to skip it," Audrey said. "Nikki is feeling a bit spicy, so we left it on the list. If you don't think you can produce a good forgery, though..."

"Challenge accepted," she said with a smile and raised her glass to clink with her friends. She hadn't felt much of a challenge in a while. This might be just what she needed to get her creative juices flowing again.

Ezra Fisher snuck into the back door of the shop hoping to avoid his sister. He owned the damn business, yet he was sneaking around like a teenager. He shouldn't have to, but he'd been dodging Bronte's calls and texts, and he knew she'd hunt him down eventually. He was beginning to regret letting her have the apartment above the shop. When he'd bought his house to have a better work-life balance or some shit, he'd told Bronte she could move in. After her divorce, she needed a fresh start. But having her live over his head meant it was more difficult to avoid her.

For him, walking into the shop was better than coming home. Most people went home to relax and escape the office or job. His job, on the other hand, calmed him in ways nothing else could.

So it was almost midnight, and he'd come back to the shop to work.

He checked the computer to see what orders they had, as if he didn't already know. He always kept tabs on orders, even though it was Bronte's job to run the administrative end of the business. He'd never thought he'd be running a family business when he started selling his glassworks, but he had no desire to do the office end. Bronte was extremely organized and made sure paperwork was filed. Plus, she loved dealing with customers. She was a people person.

He was not.

He'd happily handed over all of that to his little sister so he could focus on glassblowing and creating. He was in the first stage of creating a vase when he heard the noise.

Fuck. He'd thought for sure that working this late would give him peace.

He felt Bronte standing behind him even though she said nothing. Well, damn. If she wanted to play a silence game, he wasn't going to stop her.

He rolled the glass and reheated it, adding more color each time.

After ten minutes, she broke. "Seriously? You're not going to say anything?"

He just shot her a look over his shoulder as he rolled the molten glass.

"No, 'Hi, Bronte. What are you doing here so late?' Or 'Is something wrong?' Or even 'What the hell do you want?'"

"Fine. What the hell do you want?" he asked without looking up.

She huffed, and her sigh was loud enough for him to hear over the sounds of the flames and the fans. "What exactly did you say to Mr. Wilson?"

"Something along the lines of 'fuck off.'"

"Dude. He was offering big bucks. For some ornaments. You could've finished them in no time."

He shoved the glass he was working on back into the furnace so he could address the issue he'd been avoiding. "He started making demands about what he expected them to look like, and he wanted to make sure each piece was a unique Fisher original."

"So what? He agreed to pay two hundred dollars per ornament."

He rubbed his beard. He knew he'd acted rashly, but it wasn't without cause. "After the first two phone calls and three emails, I looked him up. Did you check this guy out? He's a rich douche who thinks he can dictate everything."

"If he's a paying customer, he can. That money would've paid for new equipment."

"I know. He's not the kind of guy I want to do business with. He pays all of his upper management extremely well. I'll give him that. But he cut the hours and benefits for all of his entry-level people. You know, the people who need the money and security? And then he's going to throw some lavish party for all of the blowhards and give them my ornaments. They probably don't even want a glass ornament, Fisher original or not." He turned back to the furnace and pulled out his glass to restart the project.

She smiled and shook her head.

"You know just as well as I do that within days, most of the hundred and ten ornaments would end up on eBay, selling for a fraction of what he paid. It's one thing to sell my art to pay the bills, but I can't be that kind of sellout." He didn't even tell her about the woman who had called on the heels of his conversation with Wilson. She'd wanted a custom piece as well but started talking about exact measurements and shit and he'd turned her away.

"I can appreciate where you're coming from, but we need to talk about increasing revenue."

"The shop is doing fine."

"But it could be doing so much better. We should hold classes."

That's what he'd been afraid of while he'd been dodging her. "Fuck no."

"You brought me in to help. Why are you fighting me?"

He turned away from her to roll and blow the glass. "Because you want to bring in a bunch of idiots who think that glassblowing is a cool hobby. Something to dabble in as if I haven't trained for years."

"I want to share your art form with people who are used to buying crap made overseas. If they see the work that goes into each piece, they might be more willing to spend more money."

"Then make a video. Show it in the shop."

"People are willing to pay for experiences. Then they'll buy products as additional mementos."

He looked at her over his shoulder and met her steady gaze. "I'm not a teacher."

She rolled her eyes in a way only a little sister could. "Yes, you can. You taught me when Dad refused because he said I was too little. And last year, when that company hired you—"

"I hated every minute of it."

"But it was lucrative. I'm not saying we turn

this into a school. We can have specific days and times that are meant for classes."

He looked up from his project, which wasn't turning out the way he wanted. He hated being distracted. Bronte had made excellent points and the additional money would help buy the equipment needed to expand his operation. "Fine. As long as you do the teaching."

"I'm not as good as you."

"You don't have to be. You're talking about inexperienced people. You have to keep it simple. Teach 'em to make a paperweight or ashtray. You want to do this, I'm hands off."

She crossed her arms and narrowed her eyes. "I'll teach if you do a live demonstration and answer questions."

As far as compromises went, it wasn't a bad deal for him. He knew Bronte had the business and his best interest in mind as she came up with these ideas. "Fine. As long as you keep it to only a few classes. I'm not giving up my work time to babysit a bunch of newbies."

She jumped and clapped. The bright smile on her face was almost enough to make him join in her happiness. *Almost.*

"Now get out of here. Your yammering has caused this vase to be a fucked-up mess. I need to start over."

"You won't regret this. It's going to be awesome. I'll offer discounts and coupons to drive people in. Before you know it, we'll have so much business, you'll need to hire an apprentice."

He grunted at her as he dropped the blob of a

vase into the recycle bin. "I'm not taking on an apprentice. I like working alone."

"And yet, you put up with me."

"Family's hard to escape that way."

"See you tomorrow," she called and made her way back through the front of the store.

Ezra watched her leave, and then went back to scoop up another batch of glass to do what he'd come to the shop to do: find peace.

Chapter Two

London didn't normally participate in the planning of a heist. It was far from her area of expertise. She understood art, not how to bypass a security system or scale a wall unnoticed. But since Mia's departure from the team, London began sitting in on the planning, even though she had little to offer. She often drove the van for Nikki and Audrey, and that was as close to burglary as she'd gotten.

If she were being totally honest, she was a little envious of everyone else. Mia had always kept her a little on the outside of the group. A member but not close enough to be part of a con or theft. It wasn't that her input wasn't valued—she knew Nikki listened to her advice on how to handle the art. And she had been a distraction during recon for their first heist. However, she didn't have the same connection the rest did. Audrey and Jared were a couple in love. Nikki and Audrey were odd best friends. And while London was also friends with them, she was still on the fringes.

Kind of like with her own family.

Curled up on the couch with a cup of coffee, London listened while Audrey began a presentation on the TV in the living room.

"Meet Harry Ross," Audrey began. "He is the owner of the Leach painting that London has already finished."

The screen flashed to the painting. Then the photo zoomed out to show where the painting was.

"And this is our next hurdle. Good ole Harry couldn't be like the rest of the dirtbags and keep the painting in his house. No, Harry has it hanging in his office." Audrey walked in front of the TV with her tablet, tapping on the screen. "This is the building where Harry runs his accounting firm."

The picture was of a sleek, ultra-modern building of metal and glass. London leaned forward, setting her coffee on the table. "Ooh...are you gonna scale down the outside of the building and cut through the window?"

Nikki chuckled. "As must fun as that sounds, I'm thinking we keep it simple. I go in as part of the cleaning crew."

"That doesn't sound like much fun."

Nikki lifted a shoulder. "It's not, but it will also be easier to get in and out with the painting. It's not like it's a skyscraper where people wouldn't notice someone on the side of the building in the middle of the night. The neighborhood is filled with clubs and bars. Always busy."

"I haven't been able to find who the cleaning company is yet. Harry doesn't own the building. He just leases the fifth floor. From what I can tell, pretty much everyone in the building is gone by seven in the evening. A few randos might still be working, but not in Harry's office. They clear out by six."

"So what I'm hearing is that it's field trip time," Nikki said.

"A field trip for what?" London asked. They usually did field trips for recon when figuring out the best way into a mark's house.

"We need to know if there's an alarm on the painting, and we need to know what the cleaning staff looks like," Nikki said.

"Tonight?" Audrey asked.

"I have a thing tonight," London said, thinking of the coupon she bought to start learning how to blow glass.

"That's okay. Tonight is just info gathering. Nikki and I can handle it. How's the tree topper coming?"

London sighed. "That's the thing I have tonight. I found a studio that offers glassblowing classes. Get this. It's with the Fishers. I didn't know that until after I booked with an online coupon. Serendipity, I guess. I'm taking a class tonight to get the basics down. There's only so much I can learn from YouTube videos. I'm hoping that after I take the class, if it all goes well, I can buy some solo time to work once I figure out what I'm doing. You'll still get both birds, and I'll learn about glassblowing."

"Sounds good. We plan to hit Harry's office sometime this week, so keep your schedule fluid."

"Me?" London asked.

"You're the best driver around, baby," Nikki said.

She nodded. Of course. Relegated to driver, as usual. Why she thought things would be different now, she had no idea. She checked the time. "I have to head out to get ready for my class tonight. I don't know how long it's going to take to drive out to the suburbs. It's not like it's right off the highway or anything, so I might end up lost."

"I'm sure it won't be that bad. You've been driving us through suburban streets for months. Let us know how it goes," Audrey said with her head down scrolling through her tablet again.

As she left, she considered what she really wanted. Was it being a thief like Nikki? Not really. Being an artist was in her soul. Maybe she could manifest herself right into being a master glassblower and creating the tree topper would be easy.

She shook her head. Even she couldn't convince herself of that lie. She only hoped that the instructor tonight was someone that she could bribe into letting her learn in the studio on her own.

That was a manifestation she could believe in because if Mia had taught her anything, it was that money makes things happen.

BRONTE RUSHED THROUGH THE STUDIO straightening up and setting up extra fans, and propping the back door open, which was setting Ezra on edge. He shot his sister a dirty look.

"I know you don't mind this place feeling a little like Hades, but we have our first class tonight and most people aren't used to hanging out in heat like this."

"They want to play with melted glass, but the heat's gonna bother them? Maybe they should stay at home."

She huffed and rolled her eyes. "We have five people coming. That's two hundred fifty dollars that we're pulling in for a couple of hours of time."

"Plus the cost of materials."

"Which is negligible because we're making paperweights. Come on, Ez. This is going to be a good move. And these five are coming in with coupons. Regular price is almost double that. I'm just easing us in to get some word of mouth going."

"Whatever. Just keep them out of my way."

"You said you'd do a demonstration."

"I know. I'll do a paperweight so they can see what it's supposed to look like and then they can go home feeling like losers because theirs looks like shit."

"Way to be positive. I'll do most of the talking. Try to keep your snide comments to a minimum, okay?"

He grunted. With most people, a grunt or growl was enough to get them to move on and out of his way. Unfortunately, Bronte didn't care. She bumped his arm and smiled up at him.

Sisters.

He turned away to continue working on the piece he woke up thinking about. He wanted layers of bright blue and clear glass curving up like a flame. This was his second attempt because the first started to look like he didn't know what he was doing.

An hour later, he was on his third attempt when he heard Bronte talking to people and chatting about their families.

Here we go. He took a deep breath and did his best to remove his scowl. If this stupid class thing was going to make Bronte happy, the least he could do was not sabotage it.

A small group was following Bronte as she talked. Clearly, there were two couples who probably thought this was going to be some kind of romantic date. He swallowed a laugh. *Let's see how romantic they think it is when they've got sweat rolling everywhere.*

In the back of the group, a single woman followed. She was tall and lean with long, light brown hair flowing past her shoulders. She wore a black tank top and jeans that looked like she'd been dipped in denim.

Her gaze met his. Bright blue eyes. As she stared at him, she flipped her hair over her shoulder and smiled.

A glassblowing studio was not a pickup joint. Definitely not a place for a customer to flirt with him. Everything about this woman was trouble—from the way she was dressed to the way she looked at him. Seriously. Who wore a tank top in Chicago in November?

Bronte stopped in the middle of the studio to begin her spiel.

Rather get than get into his project again, Ezra crossed his arms and waited for Bronte to finish. She hadn't told him during what part of this ridiculous show he was supposed to make the paperweight, but he figured it had to be pretty early on. He tuned out the words Bronte spoke about the molten glass and temperatures and tools. He stared at the group.

The woman in the back stared back. Her smile was even wider than it had been, if that was possible. He could tell she only half-listened to Bronte, as if she didn't need the information. He didn't recognize her, and he was familiar with most local glass artists. The world wasn't that big. She should be paying attention. He lifted his brows in Bronte's direction. The woman turned toward Bronte.

"This is my brother Ezra, master glassblower. He created most of the pieces in the store. They are all original, so no two pieces are identical."

A woman in front raised her hand. "What if you wanted to make a pair of matching vases?"

"Well, Ezra could get close. He's been doing this a lot longer than I have, but even then, they wouldn't be identical. Rather than being a matched set, they would be a coordinated set.

Similar colors and shapes, but not identical. That's what makes hand blown-glass so special." Bronte looked over the group. "Any other questions?"

They all remained silent. Ezra forced his gaze away from the pretty woman in the back. The last thing he needed was to be distracted while making a paperweight. Fucking that up would ruin Bronte's plan.

"Today, you're all going to be able to make your own paperweight, but before we get to that part, Ezra is going to walk us through how that works. Ezra?"

"Hey." He cleared his throat. "Before we start, it's important that you keep in mind that the furnace is two thousand degrees. The glass is hot and it will burn you if you're not careful."

As if she knew his comments were directed at her, the woman in back piled her hair on top of her head and conjured some magic to make it stay. Then she pulled a flannel shirt from her giant purse and tossed it over her tank top. She might be trouble, but she was smart and prepared. He had to give her credit there.

He turned to the furnace. "You start by taking glass from the furnace. To work with glass, it needs to stay hot, and pliable. Once you have your glass, you choose what color you'd like to add and roll it."

He demonstrated the motions. "Then you take the glass back to the gloryhole to reheat it."

A snicker behind him caught his attention. Without looking, he knew it was the woman in the back. When he turned back, sure enough, she was giggling, and the mess of hair piled on her head wobbled. He shot her a quick look and she covered her mouth. As if he hadn't heard all the jokes before.

"Depending on what color you hope to achieve, you might have to make multiple trips. Then you take it to the marver to cool it a little and shape it."

"When does the blowing part happen?" one of the women asked.

"Right now," he answered. "You set the pipe down, and working with a partner, you blow through the pipe."

Bronte joined him at the bench and blew. They'd worked together long enough that they didn't need much conversation. They worked in tandem, with Bronte giving more detail on each step as they moved back and forth between blowing and shaping the paperweight.

Another trip to reheat. "Using the tweezers, you pull the glass to give it a twisted or swirled effect. It'll feel like taffy." He pulled and wrapped the glass. "Once you're happy with the look, you go back to the furnace and add more clear glass. This will encase the color in your paperweight."

He took the project to the bench and began rolling the weight. Standing beside him, Bronte said, "Ezra is using a block—which is basically a big, wooden spoon—to shape the paperweight. When he's done, we'll use the jacks to separate the weight from the pipe."

Ezra was happy to let her continue talking through the process. It took a lot of effort for him to think about what the next step was and how to explain it. He preferred to just do it.

"Once we separate it, we put the paperweight in the annealer, where it will cool for a couple of days." Bronte carried the paperweight in her covered hands and carefully set it in the annealer. Then she turned back to the group. "Any questions?"

Chapter Three

*Q*uestions? London was about to have a meltdown. She'd done her research so she understood the basics of glass-blowing before arriving today, but she'd been hopeful that witnessing the actual process would make her feel better. However, it made everything worse.

Not only would she need extra time to allow for the glass to cool without breaking—days, not hours—she'd need a partner to help her with multiple steps in the process. She'd halfway convinced herself that she would be able to wing it alone.

While Bronte set the couples up to start the project, London studied Ezra, who had gone back to whatever he'd been doing when they started the tour. The orange-red flames of the furnace highlighted the red in his hair. He wasn't exactly a ginger, but the reddish hue streaked through the hair on his head and in the curls of his beard. He stared intently at the glass as he worked, completely in a world of his own.

Having a master glassblower as her partner would probably ensure that she'd be able to make the forgery in a timely manner. But then she remembered his grumpy expression when she smiled at him. No, he would be hard to convince. He obviously wasn't thrilled to have them there.

She continued to watch as he formed another hunk of molten glass and began blowing. The roped muscles in his forearms flexed as he turned the pipe and blew the glass. Part of her thought the whole thing should've been obscene, but really, it was sexy. Ezra was a big guy. Some might even call him burly. The kind of man who would be more likely to smash glass than make it. He was fun to watch, though.

Since the couples had built-in partners, Bronte helped her out when possible. She still needed to help the others, but that was fine with London. It gave her a good feel for the process and ultimately confirmed that she would need another pair of hands to make the tree topper.

While she worked, she occasionally felt the weight of someone's attention, but every time she looked around, no one was staring at her. She knew she wasn't wrong. It was like being at a club and knowing a guy was checking her out. And since of the men in the immediate vicinity, two were on a date, that left Ezra.

But she didn't have time to flirt. She was on a mission. She had to remain focused. At least the atmosphere lent itself to that.

She could see why someone would want to work like this, though. The noise and the heat and the rhythm—it was a lot like her place.

Back and forth to the gloryhole—who wouldn't laugh at that? It had "porno" written all over it—she worked with her glass, red and blue. She'd decided that the paperweight was going to be a gift for Nikki. The woman didn't need anything, so London knew she'd be hard to shop for. But this piece, with the hot red and cool blue, was like watching Nikki and Wade dance around each other. When they finally came together, they were perfection.

The more she played with the glass, pulling and twisting, the more enjoyment she was getting from the process. She wondered what it would be like to do this for a sculpture or drinkware. This might be a fun new hobby.

When all of the paperweights were in the annealer, Bronte thanked everyone for attending and let them know when they could pick up the final product. As the others perused the shelves of the small store, London hung behind. She needed a partner and short of finding another studio with lessons, Bronte was her best bet. Audrey had done more research on the family, and Bronte had been vocal about the money her father had lost to Benson and Towers. Audrey couldn't tell if they were the reason his studio closed, but Bronte had written letters and spoken to reporters about the scam. London only hoped that the chance to get a chunk of cash would be enough to get her in.

She considered several pieces on the shelves. They were all beautiful and unique. Some were sturdy-looking sculptures and others delicate vases. Thinking of Ezra, she couldn't imagine him choosing to create fragile items. Then again, maybe she had him pegged wrong. He, too, was an artist after all.

"Is there something I can help you with?" Bronte asked.

London glanced around. Everyone else was gone. "Hi, I'm London. First, thank you for the enlightening experience."

"You're welcome."

"Second, I have a proposition."

Bronte tilted her head and looked at her with suspicion in her eyes.

"I'm an artist. I work in various media, paint, clay, ceramics, and some metalwork. But I want to make a special gift for my mom. Would it be possible for me to rent some studio time?"

Bronte leaned against the counter that held the register and crossed her arms. "You're not an experienced glassblower. It wouldn't be safe."

London held up her hands. "I have the basics down. But I wouldn't expect you to give me the keys to the kingdom, so to speak. I would need an extra pair of hands and I'd pay you for your time. Generously."

Bronte rolled her lower lip in and bit down. "It's not something that we do."

"I'd be willing to come in when the place is closed. In fact, I'd prefer it that way. No distractions. This is a priority for me. It's a special Christmas gift." London rummaged in her bag for a piece of paper and pen. She did a quick sketch of the tree topper. "This is what I'm looking to make. I understand that as a novice, it might take me a few tries, and I'm willing to pay for the studio time."

She slid the drawing over to Bronte. On another scrap of paper, she wrote a dollar amount and placed it on the counter.

Bronte was studying the drawing. "This will take some work, but I think it's doable." Then she glanced at the second piece of paper and her eyes bugged. She cleared her throat. "Well, then. I think we can work something out."

London smiled. "Excellent. I'll give you a call tomorrow and we can schedule some times to work."

Bronte extended a hand. "I'm looking forward to working with you."

They shook and London left feeling very Mia-like, all sleek, and I've-got-more-money-than-I-know-what-to-do-with. She had little doubt that with Bronte's help she'd be able to get the topper done on time.

When Ezra heard the bell jingle again, he figured it was safe to move around without being bombarded with questions from a bunch of strangers.

He turned to start on another piece when Bronte came running in, a huge smile on her face, waving a scrap of paper at him.

"I told you this was a brilliant idea."

"I'm glad you had fun teaching strangers the magic of making a paperweight. Still not interested in teaching it for you." He turned back toward the furnace.

But Bronte stepped in front of him. "London, one of the women from tonight? She's an artist. She wants to rent studio time to make a special Christmas gift."

"No." He sidestepped to get back to work.

Bronte held up a hand. "You have to listen."

"No, I don't. My shop isn't for rent. I'm not a babysitter."

"You don't have to be. I will." She shoved the paper in his face. "This is what she's willing to pay."

He blinked as the number came into focus. Then he stepped back. "Which woman was this?"

"Her name is London. She was the woman who came in alone."

Figures. "The one who showed up dressed inappropriately and who giggled at the name of the equipment." He stared down at his sister. "Giggled."

"She handled herself well tonight. Everything about her paperweight went smoothly. It's a win-win. This kind of money will help you meet your goals faster."

"No one pays that kind of money to use a studio. It's something shady." His thoughts went back to Wilson and his ornaments and then the phone call. People suddenly wanting to pay him a lot of money left him unsettled.

"It is not. She showed me what she wants to make, and while it's more complicated than a paperweight, it's not outrageous. It's a gift for her mom."

"It doesn't add up."

His sister crossed her arms and narrowed her eyes. "So, as long as I get payment upfront, and I'm here babysitting her the whole time, it doesn't matter that it doesn't add up. We get paid handsomely for our time."

"I don't need to be tripping over a newbie when I have my own commissioned pieces to get done before the holidays."

"She already agreed to come in after close. It'll be just me and her."

"I don't like to be told when I can and can't work."

"We'll work around your schedule. Once we have a plan, I'll let you know. That way, you can avoid her." She huffed. "Anything else?"

"You have all the answers, don't you?"

"I'm good like that."

"Fine. Keep her out of my way, and do what you want."

"Yay!" She jumped up and clapped. "Make sure you let me know what days and times I need to avoid. London is going to call me tomorrow to set things up."

He grumbled. Part of the reason he loved having his own business was that he didn't have to answer to anyone. He could start his workday at eight at night if he wanted. But he could do this for Bronte. A week or two of scheduling his work time so he could avoid a woman who clearly had trouble written all over her. He could handle it.

And as Bronte pointed out, that was a lot of money for a babysitting gig.

Chapter Four

The following night, London had been surprised to get a call from Audrey asking her to come back to the apartment to talk about the job. She sat on the couch as Nikki and Audrey explained how they planned to get into Harry Ross's office to lift the Leach painting.

"Nikki is getting the uniform so she can follow the crew in," Audrey said.

"Aren't they going to know you're not one of them?" London asked as she looked at the photos Audrey had taken of the crew the previous night.

"I'm going to follow, not blend," Nikki said. "I'm going to go in after they've already hit the elevator. Running late, gonna be in trouble, yadda-yadda."

"And that's where you come in," Audrey said, looking at London.

"Me? You mean other than driving the van?" She tried not to sound too excited at the prospect.

"Yeah, you. We might need extra help getting Nikki in," Audrey said. "No matter what, I need to watch cameras. I've found that more often than not, we need extra bodies to pull off getting in when there are other people around."

"Hey. I didn't need help getting into Ingram's house," Nikki argued.

Audrey scoffed. "But you needed help getting out."

"Did not."

Audrey crossed her arms. "What would've happened if Wade hadn't been there to distract the dogs."

"I would've figured it out."

London reached over and patted Nikki's arm. "It's okay to admit he helped you. You don't have to do everything alone."

"I'm not. I rely on Audrey routinely to get me into places, and I count on you to give me fabulous artwork. See? Not alone."

"We're all a work in progress," London said.

"So I guess you'll be my distraction," Nikki said as she plopped on the couch beside her. "Security will want to check my ID, so while I'm fumbling with my bag, having a meltdown because I'm going to lose my new job because I'm such a fuck-up, you'll come in and cause a scene, drawing them away from me. They'll let me pass because I'll seem harmless compared to you."

London laughed. Anyone who'd ever met Nikki wouldn't think of her as harmless. "What kind of distraction am I supposed to make?"

Nikki squinched up her face. "Play drunk. Men are always suckers for drunk women. Then run the gamut of emotions—angry, sad, flirty, whatever. Even better if you could get some tears going. They *never* know what to do with tears."

"Easy. I can fake just about anything. But how do I get out? Won't it be suspicious if I just leave?"

She and Audrey both looked at Nikki for an answer.

Nikki threw up her hands. "I don't know. I usually wing it."

"Maybe I could pop in and rescue her. You know, be the good friend who lost track of her drunk buddy," Audrey offered.

"I need you in the van running interference with cameras." She crossed her arms and closed her eyes. Then she huffed. "I can have Wade do it."

"What?" Audrey and London both said.

"He wants to help, and he can con his way into or out of any situation." She pulled out her phone and sent a text.

"Are you sure?" London asked. "You said you wanted to keep him out of this."

"I do. But in all honesty, I think part of him is missing the action. If giving him a small part keeps him out of the real trouble, I can probably live with that." She reached for the beer on the table. Then her phone buzzed. "Wade's in."

"When are we doing this?"

"We think tomorrow night is our best bet," Audrey answered.

"I have a thing tomorrow night. What time?"

"Cleaning crew comes in around nine."

"Oh. That'll work. My thing is later."

"Your thing is a late-night booty call," Nikki said in a sing-song.

"I wish. I'm going to the studio to start

working on the tree topper." She snagged Nikki's beer and took a swig. "It's a lot more than I thought it would be, so I've enlisted help."

"Who?" Audrey asked, setting her tablet on the table and joining them on the couch.

"Bronte Fisher runs the place with her brother. I took a class last night to check it out and offered her a big payout for letting me rent studio time. I need her expertise and hands. But I have to work around her brother's schedule. He's the master glassblower, and he doesn't want strangers in his space."

"How'd you convince them to do this? The guy I talked to was pretty rude," Audrey said.

London thought of Ezra and figured he was probably the one who talked to Audrey. Rude. Gruff. Not that much different. "As far as they know, I'm making a special gift for my mom. The way Bronte's eyes lit up at the amount of money I offered, she wants the cash. And it's not like I showed her the real deal. As long as I can get the shape, I'll add the fake diamonds after the fact." She finished off Nikki's beer.

"Hey, I don't mind sharing, but damn, girl. You drank it all." Nikki took the empty to the kitchen and returned with two fresh bottles. "It's not like you to be this wound up. What's going on?"

London shook out her shoulders and tried to loosen up. "I'm restless. I don't like not being able to handle the art you guys need. As much as I think I'm up for the challenge, I'm not sure I can do it. Mia never mentioned glassblowing when she hired me."

"If you can't, you can't. We've talked about skipping pieces before. Don't stress yourself out." Audrey gave her shoulder a bump. "You can feel good even if the topper doesn't work because we'll have paid the Fishers some of their lost money."

While Audrey's understanding made her feel a little better, it was still a failure on her part. She hated that feeling. Audrey's words were kind, but they were reminiscent of her father's. He never told her art was stupid—he did have an appreciation for it—but every time they talked about her work, his comments felt patronizing. Like a pat on the head because nothing she did was serious.

Audrey would never treat her that way, but the irritation rose anyway. She wanted to prove herself. To show everyone that she was an excellent artist.

"I'll get it done. It might not be perfect, but who's going to notice, right? It's going to be on the top of a tree during a party when everyone is at least half-lit."

"That's my girl." Nikki tapped her bottle against London's. "Just has to be good enough."

London took a swallow of beer. No. Good enough wasn't enough. She had to be better than that. "Let's talk about what kind of distraction I need to be for the security guards tomorrow night. Are they at least hot?"

LONDON WAS EXCITED—NO, SHE WAS BEYOND keyed up—to actually take part in the heist. She didn't mind being in the van with Audrey because she was technically the getaway driver, but having an active role? It was gonna be fun. Nikki told her to dress provocatively. Well, Nikki's exact words were "Dress one step up from street-walker. We want the guard to be drooling and hoping for a wardrobe malfunction."

So she slid into her slinkiest black dress that could pass for a negligee and skipped the double stick tape that would normally keep things in place. Getting behind the wheel of the van was a little awkward and she knew she looked totally out of place driving the thing, but Audrey liked to work from the van. It was a mobile office for her. Not quite as high-tech as you saw on TV, but it was damn close.

She drove to the apartment, where Nikki, Wade, and Audrey would be waiting. Nikki wanted her and Wade to run through the distrac-tion scenario on the way to the job. And of course, Nikki would need to eat, as was her pre-heist rit-ual. When she pulled up in front of the building, she texted.

A moment later, all three were headed to-ward the van, looking like one hell of a motley crew.

Wade had his light hair slicked back and he wore a sexy suit that quietly declared, "I'm impor-tant." Nikki wore a light blue uniform dress and she had on a pink wig and a pair of glasses. She was also pushing a small cleaning cart. Audrey wore her usual attire of jeans and a sweatshirt. If she didn't know them, she'd never peg them as friends.

Audrey whipped the side door open and climbed in. Then she popped the back door open for Nikki to stow the cart. Wade got in the passenger side.

When she slid into a seat next to Audrey, Nikki let out a low whistle. "Lookin' good."

London preened. "Why, thank you. I do clean up quite well."

"Wow," Wade said beside her.

Nikki smacked his arm. "Stop perving on my friend."

"I was simply appreciating the view, babe. You know I only have eyes for you."

"Ew," Audrey said. "You all sound like you're running cons on each other. Let's go."

London pulled away from the curb.

"All right." Nikki clapped her hands. "I'm thinking if you, London, go running in the lobby a minute or so after me—as I'm searching for my ID —and start yelling about your no-good, cheating bastard of a boyfriend, demanding access to go catch him in the act, the guards will have to handle you."

"This is an office building," Wade pointed out.

"Of course, the lying sleazeball would have a side piece at the office," London suggested.

"And once Nikki is upstairs, I'll swoop in and apologize to the nice guards about my girlfriend who overindulged and I'll make some kissy noises and promise to buy her another diamond," Wade said.

"Ooh...I get a diamond?"

"We know what we're doing," Wade continued. He shot a look at Nikki over his shoulder. "We got this."

"Where are we stopping for food?" London asked.

"Chili dogs!" Nikki yelled.

"Don't spill on the uniform," Audrey said, sounding like a mom.

"It'll make my frazzled personality more authentic," Nikki countered.

London enjoyed the banter of her friends in the back as they ate on the way to the job. She parked the van around the corner from the building, and Audrey handed them all earpieces. London tucked it in her ear.

"These are the newer ones," Audrey explained. "When you did the first job with us, luring the dog through the yard, you had to press the button for us to hear you talk. This is automatic."

Nikki leaned between the front seats and eyed her and Wade. "That means I can hear everything between you. Everything," she added with a menacing smile.

"Are you serious? I would never make a move on your boyfriend."

Nikki burst out laughing. "I'm just fucking with you." Then she sat back and straightened her wig and uniform. "Let's do this."

The nervous flutters in London's stomach multiplied as she watched Nikki walk toward the building.

"Crew just went up in the elevator. I'm going in."

London continued to stare in the direction Nikki had walked. Audrey nudged her arm. "That's your cue to head out. You need to get in a minute or so after her."

"You got this," Wade said. "I'll be right behind you."

As she walked toward the building, London mussed her hair a little and rotated her shoulders to loosen her muscles. A tipsy woman would be relaxed. A cold wind whipped by and her whole body shivered. She really wished she'd worn a coat. The guys were in for a full view of her nipples standing at attention in the thin dress. She rubbed her arms and waited. In her ear, she heard Nikki chatting with the guard. She sounded really worried. Damn, she was good.

London stumbled through the revolving door and marched toward the bank of elevators, trying to hide how cold she was.

"Excuse me, miss."

London spun on her heel and wobbled. The guard reached out and grabbed her elbow to steady her.

She yanked her arm away. "You can't protect him. I'm going to catch him. *Meet me for drinks, babe. Sorry, I'm running late, but I'll be there, just wait for me.*" She poked a finger in the air. "And I'm just stupid enough to wait!"

"Ma'am, who are you here to see? The offices are all empty. The workday is done."

"Psh. That's what he wants you to think. He's probably up there boning her right now."

"Can I…" Nikki said.

One guard waved her to the elevator. Mission accomplished.

"I'm done with his lies. You have to let me catch him."

"Miss, please calm down. Who are you looking for?"

"Benedict Winslow."

Nikki snickered in her ear. "Nice name."

The guards looked at each other. One sat in front of the computer and typed away.

Just then, from behind her, Wade called, "Babe."

She turned around, holding the counter for support. "Bennie?"

"I've been looking all over for you. I went to the bar and you weren't there." He crossed the room and reached for her.

"You said you were coming and then you weren't there, and I thought—" She hiccupped and swallowed fake tears.

Wade took off his coat and wrapped it around London's shoulders. The warmth seeped into her chilled skin. He led her away from the guards and told her to wait a minute. He slid some money on the counter for the guards. "I'm sorry about this. Whenever she has too much to drink, she thinks I'm cheating on her. I don't even work here. Her father—a serial cheater—worked here. Sorry for the trouble."

"No worries," one guard said. Then he called a little louder. "Are you okay, miss? Would you like us to call you a car?"

"No. Thank you. Benny's here now." She

waved at them and blinked away the tears filling her eyes as she looked over at Wade in adoration.

Wade guided them through the door. On the street, he said, "Benny? Really?"

"You didn't give me a name. And Benedict sounded just sleazy enough."

They walked back to the van and listened as Audrey kept a running commentary with Nikki about cameras. By the time London had the van started and was circling the block to cut down the alley, Nikki already had the painting replaced on the wall and was heading toward a back exit.

As soon as they pulled up, Nikki hopped in with a huge smile. "Excellent acting job, London. Let's go celebrate!"

"As much as I'd like to, I need to go to the studio to start working on the tree topper."

"Party pooper."

"I'm sure Wade can help you celebrate."

Nikki bounced around in the back seat. "Aren't you too pumped to play with glass? You need to burn off the energy."

She understood what Nikki was talking about. Now that they were safely away from the building, the adrenaline rush was done, but her nerves were buzzing. She would just have to find a way to channel that energy through her art. After dropping everyone off at the apartment, she drove to the glassworks studio still riding the high of a successful heist.

Chapter Five

*E*zra set the next glass in the annealer. That was the last of the set he'd been commissioned to make. Now he could focus on some things that he wanted to do. He didn't mind when Bronte took orders for specific pieces. Those often carried the bills when art didn't. But he'd been itching to create a new piece for days. He'd toyed with ideas in his head and tried to sketch something out, but he wasn't sure exactly what he wanted it to be.

Sometimes, creating was like that. He just needed to start and let the glass show him what it wanted to be. It sounded way too woo-woo for him whenever he tried to explain it, but breathing life into glass was better than talking about some mysterious muse that might strike. He never put faith in things he couldn't touch. Blaming lack of productivity on a muse was a cop-out.

He put in his earbuds and turned the music up to drown out everything. He pulled some glass from the furnace and began to work. He fell into the rhythm of heating and shaping. He didn't add color. Not to this piece. This one would remain clear. He shaped and blew, twisted and pulled. Just as it was starting to take shape, he felt a blast of cold air as Bronte came in the back door.

She shivered and then looked at him wide-eyed.

Fuck. He glanced at the clock on the far wall. How had time slipped away so quickly?

He must've looked angry because Bronte threw her hands up and said, "You told me tonight would be good. That you'd be done and I could work with London."

He huffed in frustration. "I know. It's fine."

"Uh, are you gonna stay?"

He pointed to the glass. "I am in the middle of something here. Don't worry. I'm not gonna intrude on your studio time with the rich one."

"Good. Because she'll be here soon." She pointed at his face. "Maybe don't look so mean."

He forced a smile.

"Ew. You look feral. Don't do that either."

He chuckled and went back to work. There was no reason why he couldn't continue working while Bronte and London did their thing. With any luck, they could finish the whole project tonight, and they'd be out of his hair.

He heard Bronte unlock the front door and the barest sounds of female chatter floated through the studio. It immediately felt odd. He so rarely had women in his space. Except for Bronte and she didn't count. He turned as they came into the back and his jaw dropped. If he'd thought the outfit London came to class in had been inappropriate, this one was downright sinful.

She wore a slinky, slippery black dress that dipped into a deep V in the front. If she shifted too fast, he was sure she'd pop out. Her hair was bigger than it had been last time and her face was made up.

Giving him a tentative smile, she held up a bag. "No need to lecture about how I can't work like this. I'm just coming from a thing I had to do. I'm going to change."

Bronte glared at him and pointed London in the direction of the bathroom. Once London was out of sight, she said, "Do *not* screw this up."

"Me? What did I do? She's the one who walked into the studio barely dressed. And so help me if her *thing* had her drinking, she can't be operating in here."

"She's sober. And you're not the babysitter, remember? I am. We'll be fine." She waved a hand at him. "Go back to what you were doing. And don't ogle her."

"I wasn't ogling." He huffed and turned back to his station. It wasn't ogling to notice someone was barely dressed, showing that much skin in the middle of November.

Although he put his earbuds back in and turned his music on low—Fleetwood Mac—he couldn't help but notice when London came back wearing a flannel shirt with the sleeves rolled up and another pair of painted-on jeans. She'd also removed most of the makeup she'd had on, which made sense. Otherwise, she'd have ended up looking like a raccoon after a few minutes in front of the furnace. Bronte had learned that the hard way.

He trusted Bronte to teach London and keep everything safe, but he still kept an eye on them. Bronte was determined to get the extra money for the studio, and he was afraid she might make some bad decisions. They worked and Bronte explained how to make the shape. The first time, they hadn't gotten far and London declared the color was wrong. Bronte tried to convince her that the glowing color they were looking at wouldn't remain.

But London wasn't hearing it.

He removed an earbud. "Bronte knows what she's talking about. You won't see the actual color until it starts to cool."

"I know that. But when I made my paperweight, I used red and I knew I would need something a shade darker, deeper than that. This—" She pointed at the small globe of glass. "is lighter in color. I need more red or a darker red."

He shook his head. She was Bronte's problem, not his. She was an artist, so maybe she was right about the color. He couldn't offer more input because he didn't know what she was trying to make.

Behind him, he heard a huff and the women went back to reheating and coloring the project. Once she was happy with the color, Bronte had her start blowing. Then there was more arguing about how to make the shape. Bronte was doing everything he'd taught her, but there was obviously some miscommunication. He yanked his earbud out again.

"What are you trying to do?"

Bronte held up a hand. "I've got this."

He crossed his arms and waited as the scene in front of him unfolded.

London closed her eyes, took a deep breath, and when she reopened her eyes, she said, "The spire at the top needs to be seven inches. Then there's the twisted section and the bubbled part at the bottom. We need to go taller, right?"

"Yes, but if you blow too much at once," Bronte explained, "you'll end up with a globe."

London sighed.

"We need to work in sections. It'll take time, but it's doable."

"Okay. Let's try this again."

They worked in tandem to start again. Ezra remembered that kind of frustration. Where he could see in his mind what he wanted to make, but the glass wouldn't cooperate. Not until he learned to work with it and not against it.

An hour later, London's yell let him know that her frustration had gotten the better of her. He turned to see what the problem was this time.

"It's not that bad," Bronte said. "We just need to approach it another way."

"It *is* that bad. It looks like a pregnant snowman."

Ezra looked at the end of the rod and chuckled.

London's head shot up and she stared at him. "Was that a laugh?"

"Yeah. It was an apt description," he said, pointing to the bloated glass.

"But I've only seen you frown and grimace. That's like a legit smile." When she said it, her face brightened.

"I'm not that bad. I smile."

This time, Bronte chuckled. "Let's not show her the smile you gave me. It'll definitely scare her off."

"I doubt it. I don't scare that easily." She gave him a wink and then turned to Bronte. "There's no saving this, is there?"

"Not that I can see. You need to blow slower while I stretch and twist the spire. We're probably going to have to blow, stretch, blow, stretch, and then do the twisting. Unfortunately, we have to play around to figure out how far to go before twisting because that'll shorten the spire. You get the picture."

"Damn." London glanced up at the clock. "I don't want to keep you up all night. When can we try this again?"

Bronte looked at him.

Before realizing what he was offering, he looked at London's bright blue eyes and found himself saying, "Whenever you want as long as it's after closing."

She gave him one of those sparkling smiles again. "I don't want to intrude on your work."

He shook his head. "It's some good comic relief."

Something passed over her face. Her smile almost slipped before she caught herself and the corners flew up higher. "So glad to be of service." To Bronte, she said, "Can I help clean up or anything?"

"No. I got this. Give me a call when you want to come back."

"I'll be here tomorrow."

"Okay. See you then."

London went back to the bathroom where she left her bag and slinky dress. Ezra followed.

When she came out, he said, "You know I was kidding, right?"

She stared blankly at him.

"The comic relief crack. Your pregnant snowman joke was funny. That was all I meant."

She smiled again, much weaker than her previous ones, and waved her hand. "Oh, yeah. Of course. I'll see you tomorrow."

"Okay." He watched her walk out the door, and a niggling feeling told him he'd managed to fuck up even though he'd been trying to be friendly. Bronte had been right. He should've just stayed out of it and away from London.

LONDON STEPPED OUTSIDE AND A BLAST OF cold air whipped around her. She was hot and clammy from glassblowing, but her skin was heated from all of the conflicting emotions she'd experienced over the last ten minutes.

When Ezra smiled at her, warmth pooled in her belly—the good kind of warmth—the kind that said *maybe we should get naked together*. She was rarely that wrong when reading men. A few minutes later he was basically calling her a joke.

It shouldn't bother her. She knew better, but the added scrutiny by an expert as she tried to focus on the tree topper rattled her. She drove back to her loft and crawled into bed, but she couldn't sleep. She was a mess.

Between the adrenaline from the heist and working on the tree topper and misreading Ezra's looks, her brain was firing in fourteen different directions. She threw off her covers and went to her studio. Staring at the canvases she had set up for the upcoming forgeries, she considered working on them.

But being in learning mode at the studio with Bronte and Ezra got her fired up to create—really create something new. Something for her.

She'd planned on reaching out to some galleries in the spring to see if she could have a show. She was still a no-name in the city, but she knew if she could get some attention on her work, people would like it.

She was a damn good artist. She just wasn't feeling like it lately. Grabbing a sketchpad and her favorite pencils, she began to sketch. She drew by the twinkling lights of her Christmas decorations. The basic line drawing flowed from her fingers and before she knew it, she was onto another page and another. The sun crept up through the windows, peeking through the frost on the glass. London stood and stretched. For the first time in months, she felt productive. No, productive wasn't the right word. She'd been plenty productive forging art for Mia.

Accomplished.

She felt accomplished because this art was for her, from her mind, with her vision. And after last night's tree-topper failure, she needed a win.

What felt like five minutes after she crawled

into bed, London's phone was ringing and the doorbell was buzzing. Who the hell was bothering her now?

She stumbled out of bed with her phone in her hand. "Hello?"

"Open the door!" Nikki yelled in her ear. "It's fucking cold out here, and I've been ringing your bell for like ten minutes."

London went to the front door and yanked it open.

"Let me in. I'm freezing my ass off." She thrust a cup at London. "It was hot, but it might not be anymore."

London shoved the door closed against the freezing wind outside and followed Nikki back inside. She put the coffee down and pulled on a sweatshirt. "What are you doing here?"

"You didn't celebrate last night, so I thought we should celebrate today."

"With coffee? No champagne?" Expensive champagne was Nikki's go-to celebration ritual.

"I was going to, but both Wade and Audrey said you'd prefer coffee. How'd it go last night?"

London sank onto the couch. "Not great. Bronte thinks we can still get it done, but it's gonna take multiple tries to get it right."

Nikki stood in the middle of the room and studied the sketches London left scattered on the floor. "This isn't for one of ours, is it?"

"No. I couldn't sleep last night, so I did some drawing."

Nikki squatted and picked one up, set it aside, then picked up another. "So who's the dude?"

"What?"

"You have dick on the brain."

"What are you talking about?"

Nikki set the pages side-by-side. "You stayed up all night drawing the same dude. But is he butt ugly? You didn't draw his face once." She snickered and sat on the floor.

"What are you talking about?" London stood and took in the sketches from Nikki's perspective. She'd known she spent the night drawing men, but now that Nikki pointed it out, London realized she'd drawn Ezra. She took a long drink of coffee to hide her acknowledgment.

"Who is he?"

"I was just sketching."

"The same guy repeatedly. Is he what's got you messed up?"

"Dude, I did not get enough sleep to follow anything you're saying."

"I'm here because Audrey and I both noticed that you seem off your game. Like something's bothering you. Is it him?"

London sighed and sat on the floor beside Nikki. "No. To be honest, this is the glassblower guy."

"Beefy arms. I never took you for an arm girl."

"I never thought I was either until I saw him working with molten glass, sleeves rolled up, defined muscles." She was getting warm thinking about it again.

"So you've got the hots for the glass guy. What's the problem?"

"He's not interested."

"Okay. So fuck him. We'll find you another pair of sexy arms that are interested."

London didn't know how to explain that Ezra's lack of interest wasn't what was messing with her. She sighed again, feeling the self-pity pretty damn deep. "Another guy isn't going to fix this. It's my problem. I'll figure it out."

"We need you on the team."

"The art will be done. No worries."

"I'm not talking about the art. I'm talking about you. The last few times we've met, you've been distant. You're usually the one all up in our business pointing shit out to us."

London smiled. "You guys have your stuff together. You're all in love and—"

"Don't say you feel like a third wheel."

"More like a fifth. Or seventh if you include Mia and Logan. We started this venture almost six months ago and were all these solo people."

"But now we're a team." Nikki scrunched up her nose. "No. More like family."

London offered a teary smile.

"Ah, hell, no. You can't start crying. Let's go back to talking about hot glass guy. Should I go beat him up?"

London blinked to clear her eyes and laughed. "He didn't do anything wrong. He's got his thing and he doesn't think I'm a serious artist."

"Well, then, he's an ass."

"I shouldn't let it get to me. I know better. That's my own messed up shit. But thanks for offering."

"It's what family does, right?"

"If you say so." Her parents had raised her

and given her pretty much anything she ever wanted, but she was alone in her endeavors. She didn't have any siblings. No one who had her back.

"Yeah, I say so. And that's the other reason I'm here. Audrey says family has Thanksgiving together, so we're having dinner at Mia's condo."

"What?"

Nikki shrugged. "Audrey told Jared she wanted us to have a family dinner and she was going to do it at the apartment, but Mia can't have Logan strolling through our base of operations, so she's having it at her place."

"But she's out. She told Logan she's not doing this."

Nikki smiled. "But...family. We're not going to talk about heists. We're going to eat till we're fat and drink her expensive alcohol."

"Wow. I didn't see that coming. I thought when she walked away, she'd be out of our lives for good."

"I have that effect on people. I'm rather unforgettable," Nikki said with a smirk.

London laughed.

"Now tell me more about hot glass guy. What does he really look like?"

"He's bearded. Kind of a dark ginger. And grumpy. But when he smiles, his whole face changes." As she described him, London knew she needed to figure out the tree topper fast because her crush was getting away from her.

Chapter Six

For the next three nights, London went to the glass studio to work. Bronte was very patient with her, and they tried, but every tree topper they made was too tall, too fat, or too thin. Trying to get the dimensions just right was killing her. And it was getting to the point that Bronte didn't see why close enough wasn't good enough. London had no way of explaining that to her, so she let Bronte think she was just a temperamental artist.

Or a petulant child needing the perfect gift for her mom.

If they got this done, she was going to owe Bronte a big bottle of liquor for putting up with her.

She was gonna need one for herself, too, because she wasn't feeling herself lately. It wasn't like her to be this down for so long, especially with the holidays so close. She needed to lighten up. She loved the Christmas season. It was the one time of year that most people were actually nice to each other and didn't give her weird looks for being cheerful.

Ezra was there most nights that they worked, which was weird since Bronte had said she could only come in when he wasn't there. His grumpiness eased up some. She wondered if he was a cheerful holiday person. She couldn't imagine Crankypants Fisher being jolly.

She and Bronte were taking a break and London took a swig of water from a bottle. She sat on a stool and watched Ezra work. He was in his own world, focused solely on the task at hand. He made it look so easy.

And the forearms. No wonder she'd been sketching them in her dreams and in real life.

Watching him work, she realized the extreme patience he had. He made multiple trips back to the furnace to make minute adjustments to the piece he was working on. Patience was not something she was good at.

"He's pretty amazing, isn't he?" Bronte asked beside her.

London blinked and turned toward Bronte. "Yeah. I mean, I knew he was good based on the glass for sale in the store, but actually watching him...the precision and patience. It's unbelievable."

"You can stop staring any time now," Ezra called from his workstation without so much as a glance at them.

"You said we couldn't bother your work. We didn't ask for help or tips or anything," Bronte said.

"You staring at me bothers me. I'm not a show."

But you could be. I could sell tickets to this and have women lined up around the block. Who wasn't intrigued by a man that good with his hands?

"Sorry. I'm just trying to learn, so I can figure out where we keep going wrong," London said.

"Stop rushing it." He still didn't turn to face her, and he came to the same conclusion she had moments ago.

"Okay." Tearing her attention away from Ezra, she said to Bronte, "Ready to try again?"

"I might have one more in me before I crawl into bed tonight."

"Let's do this."

Taking her cue from Ezra, she moved at a sloth's pace, making trip after trip to the furnace. She blew part of the base, and reheated, then stretched the glass, then reheated. As it started to take shape, she tamped down her excitement. It was looking better than any of the others she'd created.

By the time she had it nearly done, her back muscles were tight and screaming at her and her arms were beginning to feel like noodles. No wonder Ezra had muscles. She looked at the topper on the end of the rod.

The color seemed right. The dimensions were on target—at least as close as she could get without pulling out a ruler. *Damn. This could be it.*

She knew she wasn't really done. She'd need to make a couple of backups because she still wasn't sure how she was going to attach the fake diamonds. That was going to take a lot of gluing. But since she knew the process, she could make more.

"What do you think?" Bronte asked.

"I think we finally got it." London smiled and straightened her back. Her muscles spasmed and the rod in her hand shook.

"Whoa," Bronte said.

"Sorry. My muscles are not happy with me right now."

"Well, let's see if we can get this off and into the annealer."

London held the rod steady as Bronte grabbed the jacks to separate the topper from the pipe.

Just as she placed the metal against the glass, Ezra, said, "Wait. You might want to—"

He didn't finish the statement because the glass shattered under Bronte's hands. London stared in disbelief.

"What the hell?" Bronte said.

"I was going to suggest rotating instead of tapping. This piece seems too fragile to handle the vibrations."

"And you couldn't have mentioned that before I went to separate it?"

Ezra stared down at his sister. "Let me remind you that I'm not even supposed to be here. You didn't ask for my help or my advice. This is your project. I was busy and didn't realize you were done until I turned and saw."

London held up a hand. The tension between the siblings made her uncomfortable. "It's okay,

Bronte. It's no one's fault. It's glass. Glass is fragile. It happens, right?"

Ezra held a hand out toward London and shot Bronte a look that said, "See?"

"How can you *not* be furious?" Bronte asked her. "We had it. We were this close to the finish line."

"If I've learned nothing else from being here, it's that failure is part of the process. I wanted to have a couple made anyway, so I have a backup in case anything happens. Now, I know the process. I can repeat it. And we've learned from our mistakes."

Bronte stared at the broken glass at her feet. "It feels so wrong."

"That's the way art goes. Sometimes you get what you envision, and sometimes things fall apart." She looked up at Ezra. "Thanks for the tip. We'll be sure to try it next time."

She stretched her arms above her head and bent backward. She groaned as her spine cracked and her muscles twitched. Then she swung forward and touched her toes, allowing her arms to hang and stretch again. When she stood, Ezra was staring at her.

"What?"

"Nothing."

She smiled and winked. "You don't like to be stared at, but you enjoy doing the staring?"

"I wasn't staring. I just wanted to make sure you didn't bust something."

"Sure. On that note, I'm going to head out. Bronte, I know you're probably busy with Thanksgiving and all, but can we do Friday?"

"Um...Yeah, I think so."

"I thought you were going to Wisconsin for your friend thing," Ezra said.

"I am. But we eat early and I can be back here by night."

"If you're busy, it's not a big deal," London offered, even as she was calculating how many more days she had to get the topper done, encrusted with fake diamonds, and handed off to Nikki to make the swap.

"My friends and I do Friendsgiving the day after Thanksgiving. We do it every year. I'm going up there tomorrow night, so I'll have plenty of time to hang out with my friends. Plus, you're running out of days until your mom's party, so we need to get this done." Bronte kicked the glass into a pile at her feet. "Although I'm kinda gonna miss our late chats and the cash you spend to have studio time."

"Aw...I'll miss hanging here, too. But this might be the most expensive Christmas tree topper made by the time we're actually done."

"I hope it's worth it," Ezra said.

"It will be. This kind of gift will have long-lasting effects."

Ezra gave her one of his suspicious looks again and London hoped she hadn't tipped her hand. She didn't need him checking her project too closely. The fewer people who knew about this project, the better.

"Okay. I'll see you Friday night. Have a good holiday. Eat lots of turkey. Get fat and happy."

"You, too," Bronte called as London grabbed her coat to leave.

For the first time since starting this project, London began to believe she might actually be able to pull it off. And getting to spend the holiday with her new-found family of thieves would only improve her confidence.

On Thanksgiving, London made the requisite call to her parents who were celebrating this holiday in Turks and Caicos. While she hadn't grown up super wealthy like Mia and Jared had, her parents gained wealth just before she graduated high school. A few fabulous investments put them in a position to retire early and enjoy their money. She'd grown accustomed to their absence and their desire to give her money to keep her happy.

She'd been able to enjoy some of their wealth, but she didn't have a trust fund. She really wanted to make it in the art world on her own, even if that meant she occasionally took on less-than-legal jobs like Mia's. She'd learned early on that someone with a good eye and hand could forge any number of things.

After packing the pumpkin pie she'd remembered to purchase on her way home from the glass studio, she headed to Mia's. She didn't quite know what to expect. Mia had kept her distance from all of them as she had promised Logan she would. London had missed her, too. But having them all together—in Mia's house no less—

seemed weird. Not weird enough to prevent her from going, though.

She took a car to Mia's condo since she wasn't sure what the parking situation would be like, and when she arrived, she was glad she'd made that choice. With her pie in tow, she walked into a sleek building that totally fit Mia. She gave the doorman her name and he sent her up the elevator.

Mia answered the door, looking as fabulous as ever. Her dark hair was pulled back into a fancy twist and she wore a champagne-colored blouse that complemented her skin tone perfectly.

"Hi. Glad you made it," she said.

"I wouldn't miss this. But now I'm feeling a little underdressed. I didn't know we were going formal."

Mia smiled. "You're fine."

"Yeah," Nikki called. "You can be dressed like a slob like the rest of us. Don't take your cues from Mia."

She laughed at Nikki's comment. "I brought a pie. It's nothing special, not homemade or any-thing, but I figured I should bring something."

"Thank you." Mia accepted the pie. Looking over her shoulder, she said, "Logan, would you please take London's coat and hang it up?"

"Sure." As he passed by Mia, he kissed her temple. "Hi. I'm Logan."

London shook his hand. "London. Nice to meet you."

Although she had never met the man, she'd seen him in pictures and video. Film did not do him justice. He had a close beard and killer smile with deep laugh lines. She totally understood how Mia got caught up in him.

She made her way into the condo and looked around. It was as meticulous as the owner herself. A fire blazed on one wall in front of pristine white leather furniture. A long glass and chrome dining room table was set for eight. Nikki and Wade sat on the couch together, while Jared, looking as wealthy as the surroundings, sat on a chair.

Mia called over her shoulder, "Come with me for a minute. I have something I'd like to give you."

She followed Mia into a kitchen that was almost as big as her loft. Like everything else she'd seen, it was pristine. And it smelled amazing.

"Before things get hectic, I wanted to give you these." She slid two business cards onto the counter.

London reached for them and studied the names. Both were for art galleries in River North.

"I know you've wanted to have your own show for a while, and my position at the museum does have some perks, like knowing people in the art world. I mentioned you to them and they might be interested."

"Oh my God. Really? I can't believe it. Thank you!" She rushed forward and threw her arms around Mia, who still stood ramrod straight.

Slowly Mia's hands came up and patted London's back. "It's not a sure thing. Obviously, they'll need to see your work."

London released her. "I know. But just getting the chance is more than I've had in a long time."

"There's no rush or deadline, so when you have items that you think would make a good show, call them."

"I will. Thanks."

"Now go relax with everyone else in the living room."

London slid the cards into her pocket and made her way back to the living room. She sat next to Nikki.

"What was that about?" Nikki asked.

"Nothing. Just art stuff. She gave me the names of a couple of people who might be willing to host a show for me." She practically vibrated with excitement, but her brain went blank when she thought about what to create for a show.

"Cool."

London glanced around and then asked, "Does Logan know who he's eating dinner with?"

"Didn't ask," Nikki answered.

"Isn't that something we should know so we don't say the wrong thing?"

Nikki snorted. "I always say the wrong thing."

"They have a mutual agreement of don't ask, don't tell," Jared said before taking a sip of the whiskey he held.

"But he's gotta assume, right? I mean, especially when he looks at us? We don't exactly look like Mia's socialite friends."

"He can assume all he wants. I don't think he'd do anything even if he had confessions from all of you," Wade said.

"All of *us*?" Nikki said. "What about you?"

"I'm a nobody. He wasn't looking for me."

"Oh yeah, I bet that would change once I mention the Carlisle."

"I was a footnote in that situation. You guys were the main text."

"Getting all fancy with your metaphors now?"

"I have to keep up with this crowd."

"Where's Audrey?" London asked.

"She's on her way. She's bringing her grandmother."

"We get to meet Gram? Yay!" London said. She'd heard so much about the woman who'd raised Audrey that she felt like she already knew her.

Logan reappeared in the living room and asked, "Can I get you anything to drink? Wine? Whiskey? Beer?"

"I'd love a wine."

"White or red?"

"Whatever Mia has open. I'm not picky."

While Logan was gone, there was a knock at the door. Jared stood. "That's probably Audrey."

Nikki leaned close. "As long as they're all busy, how's the tree topper coming?"

"I still don't have it, but I think I have it figured out. I'm going back tomorrow and I should be able to make a couple so I have backups. Do you have a plan for making the switch?"

"Not yet. We didn't want to waste time planning something that might not happen."

"It's gonna happen. I'll make sure of it. I won't let you down."

Jared led Audrey and Gram into the living room. Audrey held her grandmother's hand. "Gram, these are my friends, Wade, Nikki, and London."

Logan and Mia came in from the other room. Logan handed London a glass of white wine.

"And this is Mia and Logan," Audrey continued. "This is Mia's place."

"Heck of a place, too. It's real nice," Gram said.

"We're so happy to have you join us today, Ms. Abbott."

Gram waved a hand. "Ah. Call me Ruth."

"Okay, Ruth. Can we get you something to drink?"

"Coffee if you have it."

Logan nodded and left the room again.

"Dinner will be out in a minute. Just waiting for the last couple of things to finish," Mia said.

"You really cooked the whole meal?" Nikki asked.

"Yes." Mia looked astonished at the question.

"No way."

"Mia's quite an excellent cook," Jared said.

"I just can't imagine you in a kitchen getting all sweaty, slaving away over a stove."

"That's because I don't get all sweaty," Mia responded in that haughty tone only she could pull off. "If you're good at what you do, it's not a hardship."

"I hope Jared's not joking about you being a good cook because I'm starving." Nikki rubbed her stomach.

"What else is new?" Jared said.

"Is there anything I can do to help?" London asked.

"No, we have it. Why don't you all take your seats at the table and Logan and I will have the food out in a minute." Mia waved off the offer of help and returned to the kitchen.

"Is it just me, or is she acting weird?" Nikki asked.

"Definitely weird," Audrey responded. "She's back to being the icy woman I first met."

Jared took Audrey's hand. "I think she's nervous."

"About what?" London asked.

"She doesn't usually have people over. Not people that she genuinely cares about. She wants to make a good impression."

"When doesn't she make a good impression?" Audrey asked.

"Ooh. There's bread," Nikki said, jumping up from the couch.

They all migrated toward the table. Everyone was paired off except London, so she sat next to Gram.

Putting a napkin in her lap, Gram asked, "You don't have a nice guy to bring to dinner? Or a nice girl for that matter?"

"Nope. I'm single."

"Me, too. We can have a good time together. How did you meet my Audrey?"

"We've done some work together, but mostly we hang out at my place and drink cheap wine."

"You're my kind of gal. What do you do?"

"I'm an artist."

"Really? I never met one of them before. You make good money doing that?"

"Sometimes. And other times…well, you've heard the saying starving artist."

Mia and Logan came into the room each carrying a huge tray of food. Jared jumped up and took the tray from Mia as Logan set down a golden-brown turkey.

"Wow, Mia. This looks amazing," London said.

"Thank you." She picked up her glass of wine. "Before we get started, I'd like to thank you all for coming. I haven't had a family dinner party in…well, ever." She blinked and smiled. "I've hosted cocktail parties and galas, but entertaining a small group of people who matter hasn't happened because of my father and the repercussions of his actions. Thanks to all of you, I finally feel ready to move on with my life, and I feel blessed to have you as part of it."

Mia raised her glass and they all joined her in a toast. Then the table erupted into happy chaos as food was passed around and people talked and shared stories.

London looked around and felt more part of this family than she had her own.

Chapter Seven

*E*zra was looking forward to a peaceful day in the studio. Bronte was still up in Wisconsin and since it was Black Friday, most people were either descending on the malls or hiding in their homes to avoid the crowds. No one would be calling or interrupting him. He considered what he wanted to work on.

He still had several items to make for custom orders, so he should work on that, but he wanted to make some other things for the shop, gifts that would appeal to people stopping in, looking for a quick gift. He took inventory of what was on the shelves and glanced out the window. Bronte had been nagging him to decorate the front window with paint and fake snow to make it look more festive and draw people in.

He'd prefer to just make a display of items for sale. If he took some time today to create holiday-themed items, they'd be ready for the window and maybe Bronte would leave him alone. A couple of candy or cookie plates, some red and green vases, and maybe a tree topper.

That thought led him to think about London again. She was growing on him. She was more serious about the work involved in the art than he'd given her credit for. And she was beautiful. And funny.

He pushed those thoughts aside and began making a vase to put on display in the window. Bronte had been selling things quickly, in part due to the classes she'd held over the last two weeks. She'd been right that students would buy more from the shop.

Now that meant he needed to create more pieces for a holiday display. He decided to make a red vase and a green vase. And maybe one with gold streaming through it. That would look festive. Then, over the next few days, he'd start making ornaments that would be stocking stuffers or special gifts. By the end of the week, the window would be full. Mostly.

He worked and managed to get two vases done before late afternoon. The sun was gone, not that he'd seen any of it today anyway because the cloud cover was gray and dark. Snow was expected and it looked like Chicago weather wouldn't disappoint.

His phone rang. Bronte. "What's up?"

"Don't kill me."

He sighed. "What now?"

"I haven't left yet. I waited to see if the snow would let up, but it's really bad up here. Pileups on the highway and the side roads are nowhere near clear yet. I don't think I'm going to make it home tonight."

"Okay. Stay safe."

"London is supposed to work on her tree topper today, remember?"

"So?"

"I've tried calling her and she hasn't responded."

"And?"

"And if she shows, it would be pretty shitty to turn her away because I got stuck in Wisconsin. She knows what she's doing and she handles most of it on her own at this point, but if you could lend her a hand, that would be great."

"Okay."

There was a long enough pause that he thought he'd lost her.

"Okay? That's it? No bitching and grumbling about how you didn't sign on for this? That you're not a babysitter?"

Did he really come off as that much of an asshole?

"Since you already know all of that, and it's not going to change the situation, would it do me any good?"

"No, but not doing it makes me question your motives."

"I like the money she's paying. Letting her in tonight will make you happy, so it's fine."

"Thank you. I owe you."

"Yeah, yeah. Be careful driving home."

He disconnected and looked outside. The snow had started to fall, but it wasn't too bad here. Bronte didn't say when London was supposed to show, but given her timing on previous days, he had time to get another vase done. Just in case, he unlocked the front door but left the

CLOSED sign in place to deter obnoxious Black Friday shoppers. Maybe it wasn't good business, but he believed this weekend shouldn't be about buying and sales, so he stayed closed.

He was shaping the vase when he heard the bell jingle in the front. He paused and listened to make sure it was London.

"Hey," she called from behind him. "It's getting pretty wild out there."

He finished shaping the vase and returned to the furnace one more time to soften it before adding the final touches. "Do me a favor and go lock the front door. I don't want people thinking we're open."

"Sure." A minute later, she was back. "Where's Bronte?"

"I guess you didn't get her message. She's stuck in Wisconsin. The snow's bad up there. Accidents, so it's not safe to drive."

"Damn."

He heard thumping and rustling behind him and he looked over his shoulder to see her digging through a giant bag that he supposed she would call a purse. She found her cell phone and turned it on. A stream of buzzing began.

"Oh, yeah, she called. I totally forgot about my phone. I turned it off because I was working. A friend hooked me up with a couple of galleries and I was struck by an idea for a series that might work and I couldn't wait to start. You know how it is when you're in the zone." She sucked in a breath. "And I'm babbling about stuff you don't care about. I'm sorry."

"I get it." He understood more than most

would. Pulling the vase out, he began to rotate it to carve lines into the glass, adding to the texture. "You can stay."

"Really? Bronte said—"

"I know. I told her it was fine. Get to work."

"Thank you so much. I'll do my best to stay out of your way. I really appreciate this."

He focused on the vase but halfway listened to her setting up the station to work. As she laid out the colored glass she wanted and pulled out the tools, she talked quietly to herself. He couldn't make out all of the words, but it seemed to be a cross between reminding herself of the steps to get it right and a pep talk to not screw up.

After he finished the vase he was working on, he considered starting another project but decided that he would only get irritated if he had to stop mid-project to help London, so he grabbed a bottle of water and sat on his stool. If nothing else, she would need help at the end. He'd show her the technique he mentioned the other night.

"Again with the staring," she said from in front of the furnace without looking at him.

"I told Bronte I'd keep an eye on you. Need help with anything?"

"I think I have this part handled. It's a little tedious, but if I can remember what I did the other night, I should be good. I will need help getting it off here and into the annealer, though. I don't want a repeat of that mess."

"It happens to all of us. There's always more broken glass than finished projects. You just never know."

She rolled the glass in the red color and returned to the furnace. On her trip back for the next round of color, she asked, "Really? You don't know intuitively if something's gonna break?"

"Sometimes you can feel it. Something's not sitting right with the glass." He shrugged. "Other times it looks damn near perfect but the glass fools you. It goes into the annealer and comes out cracked or shifted wrong."

"That sounds awful. Why put yourself through it?" she asked, as she began to shape the red spire.

Her technique wasn't bad for a newbie. "It's who I am. Maybe you should ask yourself that question. This isn't your job, your career. You're doing this for what? A gift that will probably never be appreciated?"

A sly smile crossed her face. "Oh, no. This gift will be appreciated in more ways than you can imagine."

That first feeling of suspicion when Bronte approached him about this deal crept back in. As odd as it seemed, though, what shady thing could she possibly be doing with a tree topper?

"So tell me, Ezra, why did you become a glassblower?"

"My dad used to have a studio in the city. He let me come in and hang out and learn from him. I loved it. Why did you become an artist?" he asked. While he normally hated small talk, this felt natural. Not the burden it usually was for him.

She was quiet for a moment as she went back

to the furnace with her glass. When she came back, she said, "There was nothing else I ever really wanted. I've always drawn and sketched, much to the dismay of every teacher who ever had me in class. I had some great art teachers who encouraged me and it felt right. I could never imagine getting up every day, putting on a suit, and sitting at a desk. All day. Every day. Just the same thing over and over."

He chuckled. That was a sentiment he could get behind.

She worked in silence, intently focused on the glass, so he assumed their conversation was finished. She wasn't quiet when she worked with Bronte, so maybe she didn't want to talk with him. It wasn't as if he'd been overly friendly.

After blowing and stretching the glass, she suddenly looked over at him. "What happened to your dad's studio? What made you open up out here in the suburbs?"

His muscles tightened and the familiar burn of anger settled in his gut. As soon as he mentioned his dad's studio, he should've expected this question. He hated talking about it. "It closed down."

She narrowed her eyes, but turned back to her project and continued to work.

She shouldn't have asked. There was a story, but she didn't know if it had to do with

Mia's and Jared's fathers. The immediate tension in both Ezra's body and voice told her to back off. She half expected him to ignore the question. Now, she just wanted to poke, but she couldn't abandon the tree topper. She was finally in a rhythm and knew what she was doing. With any luck, she'd be able to make two or three of them tonight.

Unless Ezra got fed up with her and made her leave.

He didn't say anything more, just sat on his stool drinking his water, watching her work. The silence was both unnerving and calming, which continued to toy with her. When she had the shape near perfect, she paused to double-check the dimensions. She only had tonight. If she couldn't get this done right, chances were good that she wouldn't have enough time to get another done and still be able to affix the "diamonds."

"Hey," she called to Ezra. "This whole time of trial and error, I haven't given much thought to the bottom of this thing."

"What about it?"

"It needs to have about a two-inch opening. You know, to stick the tree branch in. This isn't going to do it."

He came around the table. "I can attach to the top, hold it there, and you can work the bottom. It's just stretching the opening."

"Won't attaching to the top screw that part up?"

He smiled, one of those rare, slightly wicked smiles. "Not if it's done right. If we use the method I mentioned the other night, it'll go even smoother."

"If you say so." She reheated the topper one last time to add some final touches. "Okay. Do your magic."

He came at her with another rod with a tiny blob of glass on it. It immediately stuck to the top point. Then he stretched his arm across and guided her hands to slowly roll her rod while he worked the bottom free.

His focus was mesmerizing, almost as amazing as his ability to multitask. His left hand balanced the new rod while his right separated the topper from the old one.

London held her breath. This was where shit fell apart last time. But suddenly her rod was free and almost bobbled out of her grip. Her gaze shot over to the topper. Still in one piece.

Ezra took it to the furnace and heated the bottom. She set her rod on the table.

"Come here," he said as he set the rod in place.

She stood next to him as he handed her a pair of giant metal tweezers.

"Just stick them in the opening and massage your way around."

She did as he said, but her focus wavered as he placed his big hand over the top of hers.

"More pressure so we don't have to heat it again."

His hand was hot and rough, but she let him guide her so she would know the feel of it, the amount of pressure to apply. Then, she'd be prepared to repeat it on the next one without his help. She tried to quell her hormones. It proved difficult between his hand on hers and talking about pressure and massage.

She took a deep breath. Yeah, this was it. She needed to do it again. It had nothing to do with enjoying the sensation of his hand covering hers.

"That's good," she said, talking about the topper as much as the experience. She stepped back.

"Go grab the gloves."

She'd seen both him and Bronte use these giant oven mitts, but she hadn't. She slipped her hands in, feeling the heavy, rough material. They were huge on her hands. She cradled them together to create a pocket for the topper to land in when Ezra separated it from the rod.

Again, she held her breath as it gently landed in her hands. She followed Ezra to the annealer and placed it inside.

As he closed the door, he asked, "So what do you think?"

"I think it's pretty perfect. But if you're up for it, I'd like to make another." She squinted and offered a hesitant smile. "Or two. Since things can still go wonky during cooling, I'd like to have a backup or two to work with."

"Work with?"

Shit. She had to get better at watching her tongue. She waved it off. "You know, pretty it up before passing it off by the Christmas party."

He shrugged. "It's your dime."

They headed back to the workstation. London stretched and flexed and relaxed her muscles. "You can do your own thing. The beginning part takes a while, as you know."

He nodded and headed toward the storefront. "Yell when you need me."

London blew out a heavy breath. Progress felt great. Being close to Ezra wasn't so bad either.

Chapter Eight

*E*zra went to the front of the store to plan the window display. Anything to get some space between him and London. His head was all mixed up when she was around. It was a constant push-pull. She asked about his dad's shop—something that always set his teeth on edge. The shop had been successful, but after losing his retirement fund in a scam, his father sold it to retire. Ezra tried not to be bitter over that. He'd always thought he would take over the studio from his dad. He wanted his dad to retire and enjoy his later years. He didn't even mind having to start all over. The Fisher name was good anywhere he wanted to go. But the company his father had sold to dismantled everything and Fisher Glassworks disappeared.

London had dropped the discussion easily enough. Then, when he helped her finish the tree topper, being close to her pulled at him in the same way her questions pushed him. Her hands were soft when he'd covered them with his own to guide her movements. For someone not used to this kind of work, she had the stamina to see it through, which impressed him. Her smile over her success was cute. He wanted to see more of it.

What he really needed was to stop thinking about the woman who was working in his studio. He'd never hit on a customer, and there was no reason for him to start now. *But is she really a customer?* The small voice in the back of his mind asked. She wasn't someone who was buying a piece of glass from him. No, she was looking to learn from him. She needed his help. So it would be even worse to hit on her.

He began rearranging vases and glasses on the shelving units. He should probably know what Bronte's system for organization was, but it made no sense to him. Even less when he considered the types of pieces that they sold more of during the holidays. He glanced over to the box in the corner that was filled with Christmas decorations. Bronte wanted the window to be eye-catching, but she'd also been procrastinating on actually getting it done. He flipped open the box and set out the items Bronte had gotten: a small Christmas tree, glitter-covered boxes, some tinsel, and a couple of snowmen. In a separate bag, she had some spray-on snow and window paint. He wasn't really an artist, so he didn't know what she thought he would do with all of this.

He cleared out the space in the front window, hoping for inspiration. That was when he noticed how bad the snow was coming down. It was piling up quickly, and the street didn't look like it had been plowed yet. None of which was a good sign for them.

He abandoned the decorations and went to the back to let London know the weather had turned. She was standing in front of the furnace, turning the glass over as she reheated it, shaking her hips and ass in a rhythm that he assumed matched whatever she had in her earbuds. He eased his way around the table to come into her line of sight to avoid startling her. When she turned back to the table, he saw that she was nearly finished with the second topper. She mouthed the words to a song only she could hear, and she still hadn't noticed him.

Ezra crossed his arms and waited. When she reopened her eyes and saw him, she smiled. Most people would've been embarrassed to be caught dancing and singing to themselves, but not much seemed to faze London.

"Hey," she said, a little more loudly than necessary. Then she held up a finger and tapped at the earbud. "Sorry. You have good timing. I'm almost ready for you."

"Seems like you're enjoying yourself back here."

"I am. Once you get the hang of it, this is relaxing."

"It's a good thing you're almost done. The weather has gotten bad out there. The snow is really coming down."

Her face scrunched up as she worked on her glass before it cooled. "I was hoping to still get one more done tonight. By the time these cool for days, I won't have time to take another stab at this before the party. I have to hope that at least one of these will be right."

"I don't know how bad the snow's going to be. It doesn't even look like the plows came through yet."

She turned the rod and studied her work. "I think I'm ready for your help."

He moved quickly to remove the topper from her rod. As he separated it, he asked, "Did you hear what I said about the weather?"

"Are you throwing me out?"

"No. But it doesn't look safe out there."

"Would it be a problem if we stayed until the storm passed?"

He took a deep breath and moved closer to guide her hands as he had for the last one, but she was already working the opening. She was a fast learner. He considered her question. He didn't have anywhere to be and no one was waiting for him to come home. Would it matter to stay?

The real question was whether he could spend that much time alone with London without hitting on her.

"Well? Can I stay?"

Looking into her bright blue eyes, wide with hope, he couldn't say no. "I guess."

Her wide smile returned.

"Go get the mitts so we can move this." She hustled over to the table where she'd left the gloves.

They worked in tandem to get this topper into the annealer beside the first one. Once it was set, he returned to the front of the store, assuming she'd start on the next one.

But she followed him. She stood at the door,

looking out at the snow falling and piling up. "Wow. It is coming down out there."

"Did you think I was lying?"

"No, but maybe exaggerating a little."

"Nope." He, too, stared at the window. At the glass itself, not the weather beyond. Why the hell did Bronte think he should be the one to decorate this window?

"Whatcha doin'?" London asked.

"Trying to figure out a display for the window. Bronte bought all this crap and it's a lot." He swept his arm out toward the boxes and the paint and the fake snow.

"Ooh...can I help?"

He looked at her like she'd lost her mind. "Why would you volunteer to do that?"

"Decorating is fun. Plus, if I'm helping you with this, you won't get mad that I'm taking a break before starting the next tree topper." She moved over to the counter and started pulling out supplies. "What do you think? Just a simple Happy Holidays message on the glass?"

She turned back to him holding red and green paint.

"Do you know what you're doing?"

"It's paint. This is totally in my wheelhouse. I've never done a window professionally, but I can handle it." She smiled. "Unless of course, you'd prefer to do it yourself."

"Have at it." He stepped back and watched her climb up into the window space. She began marking off space and mumbling to herself. "And you know you have to write backward so it looks good from the *outside*, right?"

"Psh. I'm no amateur."

He leaned against the counter and watched her work, afraid to interrupt her process, but also curious to know more about her.

"Are you going to just stand there staring at me, or are you going to actually talk?"

"I thought maybe you preferred to work in silence."

She laughed loud and hard. "I've never been prone to silence. Tell me about yourself."

"What do you want to know?"

"What's the best part about being a glassblower?"

"There's nothing better than the feel of molten glass becoming something more." He paused, then asked, "What's so important about this tree topper thing you're making?" He'd been suspicious from the beginning given how much money she'd been paying them for studio time.

"It's a special gift."

"But you seem particular about how it looks."

"I'm trying to replicate one. It wouldn't be right if it didn't match the old one. I'd feel like I didn't do good enough."

He had no way of following that up, so he let it drop, but something still nagged him about the topper. She outlined all of the letters, and from where he stood, they looked good.

"How long have you been at this location?"

"What do you mean?"

"You said your dad had a shop in the city, but you're here in the 'burbs. Seems like an odd place to have a studio."

"The price was right. Running a place like this in the city is expensive."

"Your dad wouldn't sell to you at a bargain?"

"My dad made some bad investments and lost his savings. Everything except the shop and his house. And the thing is, a lot of people were worse off than him. So when he was ready to retire, it made sense for him to sell the studio. What neither of us knew was that the rich pricks who bought it only did so to close him down. He was their competition. They sold cheap glasswork, and buying him out gave them the opportunity to grow."

She turned around and looked at him with sadness filling her face. "That sucks. Total double whammy. Didn't he look into who this company was?"

"Yeah, but they sold him on the idea that Fisher Glassworks was going to be a division of their company. Kind of like the high-end division. He figured they would keep me on as they built up more business."

"Oh, man. You were gonna work for them? And then they, what? Just fired you?"

"Yep. Closed the whole place down, and when I lost my temper and said I'd open a new shop to compete against them, they reminded me that they didn't just buy my dad's studio, but also his name. I'd been taught by one of the best, but I couldn't use that. It required some legal intervention to be able to use my name for my shop."

"People are horrible."

"Fucking rich people." The words slipped out and then he said, "No offense."

"Why would that offend me? It's true."

"Well, uh..." He rubbed the back of his neck.

"Jeez. You think I'm one of them?"

"You did offer Bronte a lot of money to make that topper."

"Okay. I'm not gonna lie. I'm not poverty-stricken or anything, and my parents are well-off, but I didn't grow up going to boarding school and doing weekends at the country club. As far as my offer to you guys, I did some lucrative work and I wanted to pay you fairly for your time and expertise. I don't have that kind of cash to throw around all the time."

"Sorry for assuming."

"I've had people assume worse than that about me." She smiled and winked. "But not by much." She turned back to the window and began coloring in the letters.

London absorbed the information he'd offered. After hearing how his dad had gotten screwed over not once, but twice, she was even more glad that she'd offered them so much money. "And if it makes you feel a little better, the money I paid you came from one of those rich pricks you hate."

He huffed. "It does make me feel a little better. How do you do it?"

"What?"

"Work for people you don't like."

She sat back on her heels in the window and considered it. She genuinely liked Mia and Jared, but their fathers and the men they associated with were the kind of people Ezra was referring to. "I look at them like a paycheck. I don't have to like who I'm working for. Plus, getting their money allows me to do other things that are important to me."

"You sound like Bronte."

"Huh?" She sat down all the way and turned to face him.

"She brought in some rich guy who commissioned a bunch of ornaments for his holiday party. Then he started telling me how he wanted them to look and dictating how I should do my job and I basically told him to go to hell."

"Did you feel better?"

"Oh, yeah. But Bronte was mad. It was a big commission that would've paid for a lot around here."

"Sometimes you can't just suck it up."

"That was my point. He wasn't one of those philanthropist types. He was all about the show, especially for his management and board. But he screwed over the little guys."

"Then screw him."

"If I'm being totally honest, turning him away was the only reason I agreed to let Bronte take you on."

She smiled and executed a fist pump. "Guilt for the win."

"You're funny." He pointed to the window behind her. "And talented. The window looks good."

"Thanks."

"I can finish it if you want to get back to your topper. I'm pretty sure I can color in letters without messing it up."

At that moment, there was something in his eyes that drew her in, and she knew it was a mistake. She was attracted to Ezra. That was obvious, but she shouldn't start something with him. It would be too complicated. "I can finish. It won't take long. You can go work on something else if you want."

"I don't mind keeping you company. You're doing me the favor after all."

She continued to color in the letters, aware of him staring at her while she worked. "I thought we agreed staring wasn't nice."

"Not staring. Just watching. Did you have a good Thanksgiving?"

"Yeah. I did a big dinner with some friends."

"No family?"

"My parents are out of town enjoying their retirement, traveling the world. How about you?"

"I saw some friends. Like yours, my parents are enjoying retirement. They usually come up for Christmas. Do your parents come home for Christmas?"

"Sometimes. Other times, I go to them. It depends on where they are." She shot him a grin over her shoulder. "Who can resist a sunny beach in December? Do you know where the green went?" She turned in a circle, looking near her feet.

As she spun back around the other way, her foot slipped from the ledge, but Ezra caught her legs. His arms were strong and warm, his muscles bulged against her thighs. She practically sat on his shoulder, and he righted her as if she hadn't just crashed her whole body on top of him. "Sorry about that."

"You okay?"

"Yeah. Just lost my footing. I usually do my work on the ground, not on a platform."

His fingers flexed on her thighs and she suppressed a shiver. *Bad idea,* she reminded herself. She patted his shoulder. "Thanks for the save."

"No problem." His voice was quiet and husky.

She took a step away and he reached over, getting close again, but he held up the green marker she'd been looking for. Her fingers grazed his when she took it. She didn't imagine the jolt up her arm at the contact, nor did she imagine the look in his eyes. He was as interested in her as she was in him. She broke eye contact and turned to the window while uncapping the marker. *Get back to business.* Maybe in a few months, when they were done with forgeries and thefts, she could think about seeing him. *Seeing him?* Where did that thought come from? She was almost done with her project. They could have sex and go their separate ways.

She cleared her throat. "Do you normally work late at night like this?"

"Sometimes. I like the quiet."

She chuckled. "Then I must really drive you nuts."

"I wouldn't say that."

"Can I ask you a personal question?"

"I guess."

"Are you seeing anyone?"

"Nope. Are you?"

"No. But I'm not looking for anything serious. I've been focusing on my art and work. Relationships tend to take a lot of effort, and I'm not sure I have the energy for one right now."

"Understandable."

That was not the opening she was hoping for. Most guys would recognize that she'd flung the door wide open for a casual fling.

"I bet you're super busy running your own business, too, right?"

"Yeah, but being the boss has its perks. I can take a day off pretty much whenever I want. Or take a long midday lunch break. I haven't had reason to do those things, but I could if I wanted to."

"That's good to know." She colored in the last letter of her window signage. Then she picked up the white and made a few snowflakes. Then she added a wreath in the corner. She hopped off the platform and studied her handiwork. "What do you think?"

"It's way more than I would've done. Thank you."

"You're welcome."

"I hope you're not planning on driving anytime soon," he said, pointing out the window again. "It looks like it's getting worse."

She shrugged. "I don't have anywhere to be. I feel a little guilty that you're stuck here, though."

"It's no big deal. Like I said, I come here at night pretty often to work."

"I do appreciate it." She stepped closer and handed him the paint markers. "I'll, uh, get back to the glass now."

He accepted the markers, his fingers brushing hers again. "Let me know when you're ready for me."

Woo-boy. I'm ready now. Instead of speaking the words, she swallowed hard and nodded. She left him to arrange his wares in the newly painted window and went back to the furnace. Not that she noticed the additional heat. She was already feeling pretty warm.

Ezra kept his distance while she created the tree topper. When this one was done, she'd ask if he might be interested in going out for drinks. Not tonight obviously, but maybe tomorrow. Or a long lunch like he mentioned. He wouldn't have said it if he wasn't interested at all, right?

She was usually better at reading people than this. She knew how to pick guys up at a club or a coffee shop. Why did this feel different?

Clearing her mind, she turned her music up and focused on the task at hand. One more tree topper for good measure. With three finished products, one of them had to be good enough to use as a forgery. She could pick them up in a couple of days and Nikki would be on schedule for making the swap.

That thought made her happy and she danced and swayed while she worked.

Chapter Nine

*E*zra knew this whole thing had been a mistake. Chatting with London, talking about his father, asking about her life, imagining getting her naked. He wasn't oblivious to where she was going when she'd asked if he was seeing someone. Unlike her, he was in a position to have a real relationship. Was he actively seeking one? No. Did he need one right now? Also, no.

Maybe for a change, he should be a little impulsive and act on what he wanted instead of what he needed. They were stuck together for the night. It wasn't safe for her to drive until the streets were clear. Maybe they could have a few drinks with the whiskey he kept in his office and see if they clicked.

He had little doubt they would click. However, his glass studio wasn't exactly conducive to getting naked, and his office only had a folding chair since he rarely spent too much time there. After filling the window display with the items he had ready and leaving space for the ones that would be ready in a day or two, he went to check on London's progress.

As she had been earlier, she was dancing to whatever music she'd piped through her earbuds. He watched her sway and wiggle. He imagined her having a similar rhythm while naked. He shook the thoughts off to focus. Going there wasn't a good idea.

He waited until she paused and looked up, ready for his help. Her gaze met his, her eyes wide and friendly beneath lowered lashes. She was flirting with him, but he still had that nagging feeling about her. Or at least her project. Something felt off about it. He just couldn't pinpoint it.

So, the faster he could get her out of his environment, the better off he'd be. He wasn't sure how long he could ignore the constant pulse of attraction between them. It'd be one thing if it was one-sided, but her obvious flirting made it more difficult.

"Ready?" he asked.

"Yep." She tapped her earbud again and waited for him to come around to her side of the table. They worked in tandem, slightly awkward, but smoother than earlier. When his hand closed over hers to guide the movements, she released a heavy breath.

Ignoring her sounds, he focused on the glass. For the first time, he studied the topper. A new niggling feeling tapped him. Something was vaguely familiar about this. Then he shook his head. He'd seen all of her earlier versions, so of course, this looked familiar. This one was better, though, in some way.

A customer probably wouldn't notice it because it was more of a feeling he had, but this was the best one.

As she held out the mitts to catch the finished product, she stared at the topper in awe. "It's damn near perfect. I can't believe it."

"That's what happens when you slow down."

"I get it. I do. But patience is hard." Cradling the topper in her hands, she walked to the annealer.

He opened the door and she carefully set it down next to the others.

After he closed the door, she said, "Now what?"

"Do you plan to make another?"

She swung her arms wide and up over her head, looking a little silly with the huge mitts still on her hands. Then she shook her head. "I don't think I have another one in me tonight."

"Understandable. It's tough when you're not used to it."

"Think the plows have come through yet?"

He lifted a shoulder. He hoped so because staying here with her when she had nothing to do wasn't a wise choice.

She dropped the mitts on the table and made her way back to the front of the store. "Shit. It looks even worse."

He followed her and looked out the window. It was bad—like whiteout bad. He pulled out his phone. "There's still an alert telling people to stay at home. Plows are working, but it's slow."

"Damn. I'm really sorry about this."

"You can control the weather? I had no idea."

She smiled. "You know what I mean. You're trapped here because of me."

"I was already here and planned to be late to get the window done." He sighed. "Bronte lives in the apartment upstairs. We can go up there to wait it out."

"I don't want to be an inconvenience. I can just wait here."

"Let's go. What are you going to do, sit on the stool for hours? You're tired." When she didn't respond, he added, "She might even have some food up there. Although, knowing my sister, maybe not."

"Are you sure she won't mind?"

"As long as you don't rifle through her shit or steal anything, I don't see why she would. She's stuck in Wisconsin because of the storm. She knows how bad it is."

"Okay. Let me grab my bag."

He studied her as she walked past. She moved much slower than she had when she arrived or any other time she'd been there. He made sure the back door was locked and he turned off the lights. "Going out the front is the fastest way up," he said when she came back carrying her coat and bag.

He unlocked the door but hesitated to open it. "The door upstairs is right around the corner, but given how windy it looks, you might want that coat on."

"I think I can last a couple of minutes. I've lived in Chicago my whole life."

He yanked the door open and she swept through. As he locked up again, the wind kicked up, cutting through his shirt. He hurried to the next door to unlock it. By the time he ushered London through, she was shivering. He huffed. "Should've listened."

"I'm fine," she said with another shudder before she began climbing the stairs. His gaze caught on the sway of her ass as she moved and he quickly looked away.

At the top of the stairs, he pulled out the keys and unlocked the door.

"Why do you have a key to your sister's apartment?"

"It used to be mine. I bought a house and moved out. When Bronte needed a new place, I told her she could have it."

"That's nice of you." She walked through the door and set her things on the floor. "I like living in my workspace, though."

"You have a studio?"

"I have a loft. The rest of the building is co-op space. Lots of artists and musicians."

"Separation of work and personal space is good. Or so I'm told."

She smiled. "That explains why you're always coming into your studio at all hours."

He locked up behind them. The place suddenly felt so much smaller than when he'd lived here. It was a studio, so standing in the doorway, you could see the entire space except for the bathroom. Bronte had set things up differently than he had. She'd created a bedroom space with a room divider. What did she need privacy for? It wasn't like he routinely wandered up here looking for her.

"It's cute," London said.

He moved toward the kitchen area. "Want something to drink? I'm sure she has coffee if nothing else. I just have to find it."

"Let me. Unless you don't want me digging around. You've been great all night, putting up with me and helping me with my glass. The least I can do is see if I can scrounge something to eat and drink for us."

He held out his arms. "Have at it," he said and took a seat on a stool at the breakfast bar. London rummaged through the fridge and came back with an armful of items. "Grilled cheese okay for you? It's an awesome midnight snack."

He looked at the clock. It was already well past midnight. "That's fine, but you don't have to cook. I can probably find a bag of pretzels or something."

"Psh. We've been working for hours." She returned to the fridge.

The sight of her bent over had him heating up again.

"Do you think Bronte will mind if I have some of her wine? I'll buy her a new bottle."

He laughed, and she spun around.

"I'm sure she can afford to let you have her two-dollar wine."

London sent him a playful look that pulled him closer. With a shake of her head, she said, "Never underestimate the power of a good, cheap wine."

With a saucy wink, she spun back around

and began opening cabinets. "Glasses?"

"Top left."

When she opened the door, she chuckled. "She only uses the bottom shelf. That's cute."

"She's short."

London grabbed two glasses and filled them. Then she went to the stove and started making sandwiches.

"What's so special about this tree topper?"

"It's a gift."

"But why this? You're adamant about how it looks and getting it done before this party."

"I've been thinking about it for a while, but since I don't work in glass, I didn't consider how I could do it. It was luck that I saw Bronte's coupon for the class." She spoke with her back to him, focused on bread and cheese.

He wanted to let his suspicions go, and enjoy the serendipity of this night, being stuck in a small apartment with a sexy woman who clearly wanted to fuck him.

But his self-preservation was on high alert. He'd learned plenty of lessons from his father, the key one being to be wary of who he trusted.

LONDON STARED AT THE BUTTERY BREAD AND melty cheese and tried to figure out how to steer Ezra away from his line of questioning. While she was good at talking to people and she excelled at avoidance, she was not a great liar. She flipped the sandwiches and thought about how to change the subject.

"Do you work in any other media? Or just glass?"

"Just glass. I prefer to be a master."

"I get that, but sometimes the same thing all the time can get boring. Other times the idea I have in my head isn't suited to paint." She pulled the sandwiches off the pan and plated them. When she set the plate in front of Ezra, she added, "Plus, I like to keep learning."

"I learn. If you want to be good, you need to not only keep your skills up but stay on top of advancements. I was in Seattle last month for Refract."

"Refract?" She sat on the stool beside him and took a bite of her sandwich.

"It's days of glassworks. Some studios do demonstrations. Then there are museum exhibits and tours. I go almost every year. Even if I don't learn something new, I see what others in the field are doing."

"So it's like me hitting the art galleries in the city. Get a feel for what they do for shows, who they like to work with."

"Exactly." He took a bite of his sandwich and groaned. "That's fucking good."

"Thank you." She finished her wine and refilled her glass, grateful that they'd gotten away from talking about the tree topper.

With any luck, a couple of days from now, she'd have the topper in her hand so she could work on the diamonds. And she wouldn't have to worry about pretending with Ezra. They ate and drank. He told her some more about growing up around a studio. The love and admiration he had for his dad were so real. It made her both angry for him because he couldn't use his dad's shop and thrilled that she was playing a part in getting a little revenge on his behalf.

Once the food was done, she was at a loss, so she washed dishes. Ezra joined her and dried them.

"This is weird, huh?"

"What is?" he asked, his voice a low rumble.

"This." She waved a hand, sprinkling water between them.

He grunted, and she didn't know if that was acknowledgment or disagreement, so she dropped it. She didn't know where she was going with it anyway. But the tension was there.

She sighed, wiped the counter down, and refilled her wine glass again. The alcohol was hitting her system now, making her feel a little looser. "If you want to go to bed, you can. I'll just keep myself busy until it looks safe to drive."

"I'm fine, but you can have the bed if you want. I think I'll watch some TV unless it'll bother you."

"TV sounds good. Got something in mind?" TV was neutral. They wouldn't have to talk because the show would keep them occupied.

"I don't watch much. Is there something you want?"

She went to her bag and grabbed her sketch pad. Keeping her hands occupied seemed like a good idea right now. She sat in the corner of the couch and pulled her feet up to prop her pad against her legs.

Ezra turned the TV on and looked at the screen. "Fuck. She doesn't have cable."

London eyed him over her paper. "Does anyone?"

"Me."

"It's such a rip-off. You pay hundreds of dollars a month for channels you never even look at. Streaming's where it's at."

"Good. You pick." He tossed the remote at her.

"It might be a little easier to pick if I knew what services she has." The look on his face told her he had no clue. She chose a service and clicked. "Movie?"

"Whatever you want."

"Yell if something looks interesting." She began scrolling but felt his gaze on her. Choosing to ignore it, she focused on the titles sliding across the screen. No horror or she'd have nightmares. Nothing sexy or she'd want to jump him again. Comedy should be safe, right? She might even get the added benefit of hearing him actually laugh.

She stopped on a couple of titles to read the descriptions. Nothing piqued her interest, so she handed him the remote again. He picked it up and quickly settled on an action film.

London rolled her eyes. "If you wanted to watch things blow up, why didn't you just say something?"

"I've never seen this. No idea if it's good." He pressed play.

She allowed the sounds of the movie to be her

background as she sketched. Unfortunately, she found herself drawing him again and that was so not a good idea. Neither was having more wine, but here she was.

She watched him from the corner of her eye and wondered if she could draw him like this. Would he notice?

"Why are you staring at me?" he asked, his gaze not leaving the screen.

"Do you ever think about going after the guys who screwed your dad over?"

"Early on, yeah. He talked me out of it. Said he made the decisions and he was partly to blame. It was over and done with and time to move on."

"Would you get revenge if you could?"

He turned to face her, ignoring the shootout happening on the TV. "I don't know. My dad let it go. It would be stupid to blow up my life."

"What if you could do something and not get caught? Something that might make them think twice before screwing over the next guy." This was definitely the alcohol talking and she was traveling a very thin line.

"Like what? Beating the shit out of them would leave marks. Don't think I could escape that."

"Something more insidious. Like steal the money back from them."

"How the hell would I do that? Armed robbery?"

"That's no better than beating them up."

"That's my point."

"What about embarrassing them? Show the

world the kind of people they are." She leaned closer, shifting to the space between them.

"Most people know what happened. My dad was caught up in that big Benson and Towers scandal. You hear of it?"

She nodded, knowing she was too close to that line again. "But they didn't take his shop."

"No. But losing everything to them made his life more difficult. He wanted to retire, so the dirtbags who bought him out saw an easy mark. He was already worn down."

She smiled. "I know someone who's good at computers and...hacking and stuff."

"And?"

"What if I asked her to plant a little bug?"

"That wouldn't get my dad's shop back. Hell, it wouldn't even get my name back." He crossed his beefy arms. "Why are you so concerned about revenge?"

"I've been reading about Benson and Towers since they were finally caught. I think prison isn't enough. They've been living in luxury for years while those they stole from have been struggling and miserable."

"This isn't some cool movie where the good guys always win. In real life, the criminals get away more than we like to think."

"I guess you're right." She settled back in her place on the couch and watched part of the movie. She had no idea what was going on, so she picked up her pencil again instead.

"What are you working on?"

"Just some sketches."

"Of?"

She glanced at him again and mumbled, "You."

"Did you say me?"

She sighed and rolled her eyes. "Yes, you. I've been sketching your fucking arms for days. I can't get them out of my mind."

"Can I see?"

She turned the pad to face him. It wasn't much to look at yet, just simple outlines of his head and chest, but there was no mistaking the bulky arms crossed over his chest.

"Is that all I am? Arms?"

She lifted a brow. "They're pretty great arms."

He reached over and held a hand out for the pad. She hesitated but gave it to him. She'd already admitted to being obsessed with his arms. Not much could be more embarrassing.

Ezra flipped through the pages, so she focused on the TV. She stared at the screen and forced herself not to look over as she heard pages flip.

"You're really good."

"Thanks."

"What's this a picture of?" He'd turned to a page where she'd been sketching the Leach painting before moving on to canvas.

"Sometimes, I like to practice my skills by copying famous art. You know, like when you go to the Art Institute and see people copying Monet?"

He nodded in understanding. She reached for her sketchbook. He held it out, but when her fingers curled over the edge of the pages, he tugged her closer. Shock had her eyes widening, but she didn't even consider pulling back.

He met her halfway. "What is it about my arms?" he asked in a near whisper, his voice rough.

Chapter Ten

*E*ven as he made the move, Ezra knew he had lost his fucking mind. She came willingly across the couch to him and he reached over and cradled her jaw, waiting for an answer about his arms. Without breaking eye contact, she stroked her fingers up and down his forearm.

"They're muscular and strong. When you're working with glass and they flex and bulge..." She gave a little shiver. "But looking at your arms leads to your as strong hands. Then my imagination starts to play with the possibilities of what you could do with those hands."

"What do you want me to do?"

"I want to feel you."

"Then come here."

She crawled over the remaining section of the cushion and straddled his lap. Fuck. She felt good.

His hands settled on her hips, pulling her snugly to him. She stroked his beard with both hands. Then she lowered her mouth to his.

The kiss started slow, a quick brush before

their lips interlocked. When her tongue swept into his mouth, he groaned and flexed his fingers on her hips.

She rocked against him and took the kiss deeper. He tugged at the band she had holding her hair back and let it fall forward. The silky strands feathered across their cheeks. He threaded his fingers through her hair, brushed it back, and then tilted her head away so he could trail kisses across her jaw and down her neck.

He sank his teeth into the flesh where her pulse throbbed against his lips. She moaned and pressed herself harder into his lap. He moved his other hand to the hem of her shirt.

"This okay?"

"God, yes," she whispered, shoving his hand up under her shirt.

Her skin was warm and smooth. He reached her breast and palmed it. Her nipple was hard through her bra. He pushed the elastic up and gave her nipple a slight pinch.

"Fuck," she said, throwing her head back and rocking against him.

Suddenly, a loud ring broke the silence. He paused, his finger and thumb still gripping her nipple.

She lowered her face. "You need to get that?"

"Fuck no." He pulled her down for another kiss and moved to touch her other breast. The ringing stopped but then started almost immediately again. They ignored it.

Then London's phone buzzed in her back pocket, the vibrations sending a sensation up his thighs.

She laughed against his lips. "That's gotta be Bronte."

He grunted as his phone started up again. With one arm wrapped around London's waist, he lifted and pulled the phone from his pocket. He hefted a sigh and answered. "What?"

"Oh my God. Is everything okay? I called the shop and you didn't answer and you weren't answering your phone. I tried London once, but if you guys were done, I didn't want to wake her because it's so late."

No, they were far from done. "But it's okay to wake me?"

"Psh. Are you going to tell me you were asleep?"

"No."

"The weather app is showing horrible snow, so I won't be leaving till morning."

"Okay," he answered, and squeezed London's breast again.

"How did it go?"

"Fine."

"Is she still there?"

"Yeah."

"Can you please use more than one word to tell me what's going on? I'm worried."

London smiled at him and climbed off his lap, straightening her bra and shirt as she did. Then she patted his cheek.

He sighed again. He'd get even with Bronte for cock-blocking him, even if it was unknowingly. He shifted his dick in his pants and focused. "We worked on her tree topper and got a few done. She helped with the front window, so it's all painted."

"Jeez, dude. She's a paying customer. You're not supposed to put her to work."

"She volunteered to paint the window."

London smiled at him. "Yes, Bronte. I did volunteer. Don't blame him."

Then she pointed to the bathroom and left him to his conversation.

"Is the weather bad there, too?"

"Yeah. We finished up in the studio and came up to your apartment to wait it out."

"Aw...Look at you being hospitable. Thank you for not treating her like trash."

Yeah, trash was not the word that came to mind when he thought about London. "Is there something else you needed?"

"I just wanted to check in and make sure everything was okay. I feel really bad for sticking you with London. I know you hate babysitting."

"It's fine."

"Do you think she's done? Will she need more time?"

"We'll know in a couple of days, but it looks good."

"Damn."

"What?"

"I was hoping she'd need more sessions. She pays well."

He chuckled. "Drive safe. I'll see you tomorrow."

He disconnected and tossed his phone on the table next to London's notebook. He started flipping through it again. She was talented. He landed on a sketch of the tree topper.

That nagging feeling came back. While they were working on it, he was too concerned with helping her get it right that he didn't pay much attention to how it looked. But now, looking at the sketches, one in black and white and then another in full color, he couldn't help but feel like he should recognize it.

"Everything okay with Bronte?" London called from behind him.

"Yeah. She was calling to make sure I didn't scare you off."

"If that's what you were going for, you were way off the mark." She smiled and then pointed at the window. "It's cleared up and the streets look okay, so I think I'm going to head out before there's a second wave."

"Oh. Okay." He stood and rubbed the back of his neck. "Look. If I misread anything—"

"Absolutely not. I was totally on board with everything. We got a little carried away, but it was worth it." She came closer and stroked his beard again. "I enjoyed it so much that I'd love to have an encore. Maybe on a day when we're not in your sister's apartment."

He smiled. "The location should probably bother me more, but it doesn't."

She moved through the room gathering her things. She ripped a piece of paper from her pad and scribbled on it. "Here's my number—address and phone. Give me a call if you decide you want to continue."

He took the paper from her and tucked it in

his pocket. After she shoved the pad in her bag and turned around, he pulled her close again. "I'll definitely call."

Lowering his mouth, he kissed her again. In the back of his mind, he thought about how soon would be too soon to call her. When they broke the kiss, her eyes were lust-filled and he knew he wouldn't be waiting long to reach out.

"I'll call you when your toppers are ready."

"Or I could just swing by." She held onto his belt loops and tugged until they collided again.

"Probably not a good idea. Bronte will skin me if she thinks I took advantage."

"Good point. Plus, the studio isn't conducive to getting naked."

"Hmm-mmm." Thoughts of getting her naked raced through his mind and he did what he could to quell them. Stepping back, he looked her up and down. "You don't drive some little bitty car, do you? Plowed or not, it wouldn't be safe to drive something like that out there."

"I have a van, but thanks for checking." She smiled sweetly and pulled her coat on.

London wasn't quite sure why she suddenly felt the need to escape this room. She didn't regret kissing Ezra, but given how much she had going on right now, she couldn't risk him finding out about the forgery. He was asking a lot of questions and part of her felt like maybe he was suspicious.

Or maybe her imagination was running wild again. Even if he was suspicious about what she was making, the likelihood of him piecing together anything was slim.

"I'll walk you out," he said, shrugging into his coat. "I need to make sure the lot has been plowed anyway. Otherwise, I have to call to remind them we should be on their route."

"Thank you." She walked out of the apartment and waited while he locked up.

When they got to the bottom step, he said, "We can cut through the shop and go out back. It'll put you a little closer to the lot."

She glanced outside at the swirling snow. It wasn't falling as fast as it was earlier, but there were still flurries. The street in front looked clear, though, so she took that as a sign.

They went out and then back through the studio, London shaking off the snow as she walked. The back door led to the alley, but she could see the van. They walked in silence to the lot. She eyed the pile of snow on top of the van and decided she would let wind and gravity do their thing and knock it off as she drove.

The lot had been cleared at least once as evidenced by the tracks from the plow that left streaks of snow in its wake. She opened the passenger door and reached over to start the engine to warm it up. She pulled out her snowbrush and began clearing the windows. "I got this," she said to Ezra, who was looking at the van.

"Interesting choice of vehicle."

"It's my friend's. She uses it for some jobs, but she doesn't have a place to park it. My loft comes with a parking space, so I get to use the van whenever."

"It looks like a kidnapper van."

London laughed, the sound echoing down the alley. "Everyone knows the pedophile kidnapper vans are white, not black."

That pulled a small smile from him. She really liked him with a smile on his face. Walking back around the van, she said, "Tell Bronte I said hi."

He followed her to the driver's side and waited for her to climb up into the seat. "Drive carefully."

She turned her body because she didn't want him to see the back of the van. It might not look like much, but it wasn't empty. Even without Audrey's equipment, it was clearly a mobile office. She leaned off the seat.

"Thanks for all the help," she said, pressing toward him for one more kiss.

"Any time."

"Liar. You hate having people in your studio."

"You've grown on me." He moved in and kissed her. His lips were cold and his beard bristled against her skin.

They spent a moment locked in a kiss, and then he pulled away. He closed her door and tapped it to say goodbye.

She smiled and waved at him as she pulled out and drove home. The streets were empty except for the salt and plow trucks. The loud scraping of the plow and the pinging of salt as it was being scattered became the background for her thoughts.

She couldn't believe that Ezra had kissed her. For days, she'd thought he couldn't stand her. Then, when he showed a little interest, he backed off. She'd never been a huge fan of beards, but the feel of Ezra's scraping against her neck as she practically rode him made her one. God, she was getting all hot just remembering.

By the time she pulled into the garage at home, all she wanted to do was turn around and finish what they'd started. But Ezra would've gone home by now and she didn't know where home was, so she'd suck it up and wait a couple of days for her toppers. Then she could see him again.

Although she should be exhausted, she didn't want to go to bed. She'd just end up thinking about Ezra, and that wouldn't be conducive to sleep. Instead, she opened her laptop and turned on the TV to an old movie. While the video played, she reopened her sketch pad to the pages that held her drawings of the next two paintings she needed to complete.

Both the Casey and the Taggert paintings were nature scenes. She didn't know either artist, so she knew nothing about their style or methods. So, she practiced the layout and format for the paintings. She reopened the tabs she had in her browser window for each artist. It might not have been the most efficient way to work, but London found that when doing the forgeries, she couldn't focus on only one at a time.

Something about copying work bored her.

Mia had never questioned her process, but now that they were switching up who they were going after, she fell behind.

She looked up the tree topper again to try to find more information about how Maxwell created the topper covered in diamonds. Who would've thought a diamond-encrusted tree topper was a good idea? He had been a French artist who had started in jewelry and a few years into his career, he started dabbling in glass. The topper was the culmination of both his worlds. He only created the one, on commission for a wealthy American businessman. Figured.

No matter what, it always came back to rich assholes.

The story was pretty fascinating. Maxwell had created the topper, but the client wanted something more spectacular, as it was a gift for his wife. Maxwell suggested the diamonds. The artist hand-delivered the topper to New York. After the first Christmas, Bradford, the owner, had lent it to a museum exhibit, where it garnered attention.

Maxwell had been flooded with interviews, which caused him to flee the limelight. He only did one interview and then he pretty much became a hermit. London couldn't find any information about how he affixed the diamonds.

Jared had procured some really good-looking zirconia for the project, but she couldn't just slap them on and hope they stayed put. And there was no way she had time to figure out how to press them into the glass while it was hot. Even if she could, that would definitely raise some red flags with Ezra.

Her phone buzzed on the couch next to her. The only person who ever called her in the middle of the night was Nikki, so she didn't even look at the screen before answering. "Hey, babe."

"Babe, huh?" Ezra's deep voice rumbled across the line.

She yanked the phone away and saw that there was only a number on the screen. "Uh, hey. Sorry. Thought you were someone else."

"Someone you call babe."

"My friend Nikki. She's the only one who ever calls me in the middle of the night."

"Sorry to disappoint."

She shifted on the couch and set her laptop on the table. "No disappointment at all."

"I just wanted to call to make sure you made it home safely."

"Yep. Streets were pretty clear. No one was out, so it was me and the salt trucks."

"Glad you got there okay."

Heavy silence sat between them.

"I had fun tonight," she finally said. "I'm gonna miss late nights in the studio."

"You can always come back. Make some other hideous thing."

She gasped. "Hideous?"

"It's a red phallic tree topper."

She fell into laughter. For a guy who didn't talk much, when he had something to say, he let loose. "Tell me how you really feel."

"It's not like you designed it, right?"

"Still. Something tells me that even if I had designed it, you would tell me if it was ugly."

"I can be honest to a fault. It was how I was raised."

"Then tell me honestly—why were you so mean to me when we first met?"

"I wasn't mean. You were with a group of people that Bronte had organized. As you know, I don't like people in my space." He took a deep breath. "And then, there you were, with your long hair and inappropriate clothes. Laughing and flirting."

"Inappropriate clothes?"

"You wore a tank top to play with melted glass."

He had a point, but... "I wore a flannel over it."

"After you were eyeing me."

"Hm. I didn't think I was that obvious. But in my defense, you were distracting. All those forearms..."

He chuffed. "You make it sound like I'm an alien with ten arms."

"Mmm...imagine what you could do with ten arms. You were pretty talented with just two."

"Why'd you leave?"

"I didn't think it would be good to spend the night in your sister's apartment. But I gave you my address. Stop by whenever you want. I am more than happy to pick up where we left off."

"I'm already in bed. Are you free tomorrow night?"

London's heart raced. She'd expected him to wait until their business was done. "I can be."

"Do you want to go out?"

"Why don't you come over and we'll order in?"

Silence met her question.

"Ezra?"

"I'm here. I'm trying to decide if you're just using me for my forearms."

"Would it be a deal-breaker if I was?"

"Not really."

"I told you earlier that I'm not looking for a relationship. Work stuff is keeping me super busy and I need to focus on that. But I like you and I want to sleep with you."

"I can live with that. Call me when you're free."

"I will." She smiled, even though he couldn't see it. "Good night."

"Night. Sleep well."

She wasn't sure she'd be sleeping well given that he'd be starring in her dreams again. One more night. She could make it.

Chapter Eleven

$\mathcal{W}$ay too early the following morning, London's phone was ringing again. She slapped her hand at it to make it stop. Without opening her eyes, she fumbled to press the button to answer. "Yeah?"

"What the hell, London? I've been calling for like an hour."

Nikki yelling in her ear was not how she wanted to start any day. She cringed and held the phone away from her ear. When the yelling subsided, she asked, "What do you want?"

"Dude. It's almost noon. Are you still in bed?"

"No." London pushed up off the couch where she'd fallen asleep. Technically not bed. "I worked on the topper really late last night and then got stuck by the snow."

"Is it done?"

"I think so, but I won't know for another day or two. Why are you calling?"

"Oh, yeah. We need you for a party tonight."

"Huh?"

"Audrey just found out that Walter Peters is having a Christmas party. Mia is slacking in getting us intel."

"Mia isn't supposed to be doing anything anymore, remember?"

"Yeah, but she could've mentioned being invited to the party."

"Wasn't Jared invited?"

"No. But Audrey added our names to the list. We're going in as a couple."

London glanced around her room, wishing for coffee to magically appear. "Why am I going?"

"These people have seen Audrey with Jared. If he hasn't been invited, they would question her showing up."

"Why can't you go alone?"

"We agreed to use the buddy system." Nikki's voice sounded as if she was reciting from a manual. Which she probably was. Between Audrey and Wade, Nikki always had someone telling her to be more careful. "Besides, if I need a distraction so I can get closer to the Taggert painting to check it out, you're it."

She sighed. She'd wanted to be included more, right? She should be overjoyed. But she was too tired to think. "Fine. Is the same black dress I wore when you took the Leach okay or do I need something fancier?"

"Dress should be good, but don't be sloppy. This one isn't a wardrobe malfunction kind of party." Nikki giggled. "Unless we turn it into one."

"No!" Audrey yelled from the background. "Low profile."

"Got it. When time are we going?"

"I think we should get there around eight-thirty or nine. Party will be in full swing and people will be too buzzed to pay attention to the fact that no one knows us."

"But it won't be so late that we look like party crashers," London mumbled.

"Exactly."

"Fine. Call me later. I'm going back to sleep." She dropped the phone and stretched back out on the couch. She should go upstairs to bed. But that required a level of effort she didn't have.

At some point in the afternoon, London rolled off the couch and made herself a bowl of cereal. While she chomped on the chocolate crunchies, she suddenly remembered her date with Ezra. If she could call it a date. She shot him a text.

Something came up and I have to go with a friend to a party.

Too bad.

I can text when I get home, but it might be late.

I'll be around.

See? This was what she liked about keeping things loose. He wasn't going to try to make her feel guilty for having to change their plans. And he was still on board for a hook-up. She spent some time working on the paintings they needed for upcoming jobs, but she was still distracted. Maybe seeing the real thing up close might inspire something in her.

Before she knew it, it was time to get ready for the party with Nikki. She decided that instead of the slinky black dress, she'd wear a gold one that she'd gotten on vacation with her mother one year. She scooped the sides of her hair up and let the back trail down. A full makeup routine covered what was left of the dark circles under her eyes from lack of sleep. Turning in front of her mirror, she knew she looked good.

Nikki was picking her up in a rideshare since a big black van would look a bit suspicious. With her phone tucked into a tiny clutch, she headed out to meet Nikki.

The door of the small silver car popped open and Nikki yelled, "Oh girl, you're hot!"

London smiled and waved her friend over.

"That dress makes a statement."

"Is it too much?"

"Uh-uh. It's perfect. People won't be able to keep their eyes off you."

"That's not the low profile that Audrey was talking about."

"Sure it is. You're just an amazingly beautiful woman. You think they're going to pay attention to specifics?"

"You talk like you're not as beautiful."

"Well, thank you, but I know how to play a role. I can blend in anywhere. Go unnoticed."

London leaned closer. "Do we need comms for this trip?"

"I have them in my purse. Audrey insisted. She hates feeling left out. But I'm not worried about running into problems."

They rode in silence from the city into the north suburbs. Even though traffic wasn't too heavy, the trip took a while. London couldn't imagine having to make this trip every day. Nikki tapped a rhythm against the armrest of the door. Even though she appeared calm, London knew her friend was a riot of energy below the surface.

The car pulled up at the Peters' house. Christmas lights twinkled around the perimeter of the house on the trees in the front and side yards. From the street, she could see a huge Christmas tree lit in the picture window.

"Pull into the drive," Nikki directed.

The driver pulled in behind a long line of cars.

"Wow," London said as Nikki handed her an earpiece. When Nikki didn't say anything, London asked, "Isn't it amazing?"

"Eh. You've seen one rich douche, you've seen them all. You'll see when we get inside. It's all bling and no personality. They live their whole lives with a 'Look at me' attitude. There's nothing beautiful or amazing about it."

London gave a stiff nod. She hadn't spent much time among the wealthy. Sure, she mingled at art galleries, but she wasn't invited to go into their homes. It all just seemed like so much.

Impatient as always, Nikki opened the door. "Come on."

"Really?" London asked as the cold air swept in.

"The sidewalk and driveway are clear. Rich people don't tromp through snow. Waiting in this line'll take forever."

London climbed out of the car and inserted the comm.

"When we get inside, just act aloof."

"Aloof?" she asked.

"Yeah. Be a little snooty. Stick your nose in the air. It'll give you an air of mystery."

"Sounds like I'm just being a bitch."

"Yeah, that too." Nikki smiled and bumped her shoulder.

London followed Nikki through the door and a blast of warm air washed over her. A skinny dude was holding a clipboard in the foyer, looking like a maître de. Nikki smiled and pointed a finger at his list, offering her phony name for the night.

Turning slightly, she grabbed London's hand and tugged her forward. "And this is Jillian, my plus-one."

He scanned down the list and then said, "Please enjoy your evening."

Still holding her hand, Nikki led the way into the living room that looked more like a ballroom. Nikki released her in order to snag a couple of glasses of champagne from a passing waiter. As she sipped, she said, "It's a little weird not having Jared in my ear yelling at me about getting drunk."

Over the comms, London heard Audrey's laugh.

"I can go grab him if you want."

Nikki just rolled her eyes.

"So what do we do?"

"We have to mingle a little so that it doesn't look suspicious. If we go charging into the library when no one else is there, someone might take notice."

"Let's stroll around and see if people are

there." London took a sip from her glass. "Damn. That's some good shit."

"One of the few perks of coming to these things."

"Think I can make friends with the caterers and walk out with a bottle?"

Nikki snickered as Audrey gasped. "You are such a bad influence on everyone."

"Me? I did nothing," Nikki scoffed.

They meandered through the crowd, smiling and nodding politely. Every time a man seemed to take an interest, Nikki slid an arm around London. It was enough to get them to back off.

"This way," Nikki murmured. The library door was open, but it didn't look like anyone else from the party had drifted in there. "You're my lookout."

"What exactly does a lookout do?"

"Watch for people and distract them so I can do my thing."

Chatting people up was something she was good at. It brought her back to the first job she had done with Nikki and Audrey. All she had to do was talk with a maid after chasing a dog across a lawn.

At least there, though, she had a reason. Standing in a hallway without someone to talk to looked suspicious.

As if reading her mind, Nikki's voice whispered through the comm, "It'll be fine. Smile pretty."

So, she did as she was told. In her ear, Nikki mumbled, "I hope you all know how much this still goes against my thieving heart. To have my hands on this painting and leave it."

London snickered. She'd heard the same version of this comment from Nikki repeatedly on many jobs.

Nikki had been in there a couple of minutes when a man started pulling a woman down the hall. He looked vaguely familiar, but London had no idea where she might know him from. She straightened as the woman swatted at the man. She clearly had had too much to drink.

"Let go of me," the woman sputtered.

"Is everything all right?" London asked.

"It's fine. Thank you. I'm just helping my wife to bed." He looked around the hall. "This part of the house isn't open for the party."

London smiled again. "I just finished a call. It's a bit chilly outside to try to talk." Turning her attention to the woman, she asked, "Is this your husband?"

The woman rolled her eyes. "Unfortunately, yes."

"All right then. Just wanted to make sure you were okay." As the conversation registered, London realized the man looked familiar because he owned the damn house and the painting Nikki was messing with right now.

"What kind of party do you think I throw, miss?"

"One can never be too careful, Mr. Peters."

He eyed her suspiciously but said nothing as he returned to his previous task of whisking his wife off to bed.

Once they were out of her line of sight, she

stuck her head in the doorway to the library. "Ready?"

Niki popped out from behind the door. "Yeah. I was just waiting for them to leave."

"I think we need to get out of here before he comes back and starts asking more questions."

Nikki waved. "It's fine. I mean, next time, you might want to pay closer attention to the dossier that Audrey puts together. Then you might've recognized his wife."

"But if I hadn't questioned her, he might've wanted to talk more to me instead of just being offended."

"Good point," Nikki admitted. "It didn't sound like a ploy."

"Oh, it wasn't. I started talking to him before I realized who he was and then I had to go all in."

Nikki laughed. "Our ride should be here in a minute. I might just make a thief out of you yet."

"No thanks. I'm good with my art."

Nikki handed her another glass of champagne. "Drink up."

She gulped the champagne and pulled out her phone as they headed to the door. It was still early enough that Ezra might be willing to make the trek to her.

Just left the party. I should be home within 30 if you're still up. Or we can meet at a bar or something

I'm up. I'll come to you.

See you soon.

"Who are you texting that has you smiling like that?" Nikki asked.

"Ezra. We had plans that I had to postpone because of this."

"Is this hot glass guy?"

"Yes."

The car pulled up in front of the house and they got in.

"So this is a thing?"

"Not a thing. A hookup. Kind of. I like him, but I told him I'm not looking for a relationship or anything serious. So, we're gonna have some fun."

"That was a long explanation for a booty call. You sure it's not more?"

"No. What else could it be? We've known each other like a couple of weeks."

Nikki shrugged. "You seem pretty into him. That's all I'm saying."

London shook her head. She was *not* getting hung up on a guy she barely knew.

EZRA HAD SPENT THE DAY WORKING ON PIECES that would go in the store for holiday gifts. Bronte had gotten home and tried grilling him on what happened with London. He simply said they had plans to go out tonight. His sister seemed a little giddy over him getting a date. He wasn't sure what that said about his dating life, but it wasn't good.

And then London canceled. He tried not to read too much into it. Shit came up all the time. He'd worked past dinner and then decided to just go home. He showered and had pretty much given up on London, so he considered his food options. Because he hadn't gone grocery shopping, he didn't have much, so peanut butter and jelly it was.

Just as he was about to turn on the TV, his phone buzzed with a text from London inviting him over. Before he could think twice, he grabbed his keys and headed out.

As he drove through the mostly clear streets of the city, he considered why he was doing this. It wasn't like he couldn't get laid. Even with as much of a hermit as he was, he knew how to go out and meet women. But there was something about London that continuously tugged at him.

She was almost always smiling. Even when she was frustrated that the glass wasn't cooperating. Her energy matched Bronte's, but in his sister, he found it kind of annoying. London made him want to lean in and smile with her.

Which was its own kind of irritating. In general, women didn't have that effect on him. London was intriguing, though. Even though it was Saturday night, there was minimal traffic, so he made good time. She'd mentioned that she lived in a big loft. He slowed to a crawl on her block. Parking on the street was nonexistent.

His phone bleeped with another text from London letting him know there was visitor parking in the lot behind the building. He turned the corner and found a spot. Then, he called her.

"Hey, I'll be pulling up front in a minute. How far are you?" she asked.

"I just parked."

"Wow. You made good time. Hang tight."

"I'll meet you out front."

"See you soon."

He climbed out and locked up his car and walked down the side of the building to get to the front. He huddled into his coat against the cold and questioned his sanity for saying he'd wait out here. But then a car pulled up.

When the door opened and London stepped out, his tongue nearly hit the street. The dress she wore was gold and shimmery and slid over her curves like water. When her eyes met his, her whole face lit up. He crossed the space between them to offer her a hand over the slick sidewalk.

From inside the car, another woman said, "Hey, there," and smiled at him.

"Hi."

"See you later," London said.

"Oh, yeah you will," her friend responded. "I get the pictures now."

"Go home."

Her friend winked and closed the door.

"You don't have a jacket?" he asked. How was she not freezing?

"We went from door to car, car to door. Plus, a coat would ruin this fabulous look."

"You look amazing, but let's get inside before you turn into a popsicle."

Her smile widened. "If I'm a popsicle, you might want to take a lick."

"I want to do that anyway." He put an arm around her and pulled her close, allowing her to take some of his warmth as they walked up the sidewalk to her door. She took a key out of her impossibly tiny purse and unlocked the door.

Once inside, he was bombarded with noise. "What the hell?"

"I thought I told you I live in a co-op. We have artists and bands. There's usually someone working on something."

"Do they all live here?"

"Um. No. Not really. They kind of come and go. Most of them aren't permanent."

It made him wonder why she was permanent. Why she chose to live here.

"This way," she said, tugging him down the hall. She unlocked another huge metal door.

"Wow." The space was pretty big. Totally open concept. She had easels and canvases and supplies everywhere. A ragged couch sat against one wall with a coffee table. But the rest of the space was clearly dedicated to art.

"Let me take your jacket."

He took his jacket off and handed it to her. He went to one of the easels and studied the sketch on the canvas. It was little more than circles and lines.

"Do you want something to eat or drink?"

"I'm good." He tore his gaze away from her workspace and refocused on her. "You are fucking beautiful."

Her face softened as she stepped closer. She reached up and stroked his beard. Everything about her was so beautiful, he was afraid to touch her. Like a perfectly-formed piece of glass. She looked delicate, even though he knew better. He'd touched the toned muscles of her body.

The fluidity of the dress was deceiving. With

a hand on his shoulder, she removed her shoes, which dropped her a couple of inches in height.

"My bedroom's upstairs," she whispered. "We better hurry. It's pretty warm in here and you don't want your popsicle to melt."

"At least not until I get to fully enjoy it."

She turned and he followed as she led the way up the metal stairs. The bedroom—if you could call it that—was more open space. She stood in front of the bed and slid the straps of her dress off her shoulders. With a little shimmy, the dress pooled at her feet. She wore nothing but a small pair of flesh-colored panties. She crooked her finger and he moved in.

He skated his hands over her smooth skin and cupped her jaw to angle her face for a kiss. He touched his lips to hers and licked into her mouth slowly. She moaned and pressed her body against his. If they were going to keep this casual, he was going to make sure he enjoyed every moment he had with her.

"Too many clothes," she murmured against his lips.

"No rush," he responded. Then he picked her up and laid her back on the mattress before kissing his way down her body. He hadn't exaggerated when he said he wanted to lick her all over. This would be a night they'd both remember.

Chapter Twelve

Sometime in the middle of the night, London shifted to roll over, but something heavy was on top of her. Ezra's arm had her pinned at the waist and his leg weighed down hers. Having sex with Ezra had been a nice break. Between that and her outing with Nikki, she was feeling more like herself. She carefully slid out from under Ezra and pulled on a T-shirt.

The room was too dark to see much more than his hulking form taking up more than his share of the bed. His share? She needed to stop thinking like that. If she was lucky, she might get lucky with him another time or two, but then they were back to their regular lives.

Like she'd told Nikki, she barely knew him. The little voice in her head told her that some of the conversations she'd had with him over the last few days were more meaningful than many of the ones she had with her own family. But it shouldn't matter. She couldn't start a relationship until they were done with the forgeries.

Look what happened with Mia falling for an outsider. She had to walk away from her plan. While London enjoyed the money she made from this project, and technically, she could walk away easier than Mia had, she wanted to see it through. She wanted to make these men suffer at least a little, even though she didn't know anyone personally affected by the scheme.

She poured herself a cup of wine and sat on the floor with her pencils and sketchpad. Since Ezra was asleep, she put on her headphones and went to work. Just to get it out of her system, she allowed herself one full drawing of Ezra. She sketched fast, her pencil scratching the paper.

She drew him standing in her bedroom staring at her when she'd dropped her dress. The look on his face was raw and real. More than attraction and when he began to touch her, she felt worshipped. One drawing quickly spun into two because she wanted to capture his body in its naked glory. When she'd thought of him as beefy, it was an apt description.

He wasn't the toned, defined muscles of models; he was slabs of steel bulky under his skin. He'd played her body like she was a blob of glass. He'd worked her over until she was molten and pliant.

Once that was out of her system, she got to the real work. She had to get the Taggert and Casey paintings done. Given that Nikki had cased out the Peters' house to check on the Taggert, London guessed that would be their next job.

And the tree topper, of course. With any luck at least one of her reproductions would come out of the annealer in one piece. Bruce Moore's party was next weekend. She'd have to move fast to get the fake diamonds on the topper.

For now, she turned her attention to Taggert's nature scene. Taggert was one of those artists who painted heavy. Thick paint in muted colors, applied with a knife instead of a brush. She'd done her research and knew enough about Taggert's style to start, but she'd been procrastinating.

Time to just start. She got out her tubes of acrylic paint and mixed the colors she'd need. She had an image of the original on her tablet on the table beside her easel. As she began applying the paint, she had to remind herself to be patient and not make it too thick on the first pass. Doing so might make it impossible to fully dry.

She had no idea how long she worked but movement from the corner of her field of vision caught her attention. She yanked off her headphones as Ezra walked up, wearing nothing but his jeans. Unbuttoned.

"Sorry. Did I wake you?" she asked.

"No. It was so quiet I thought you snuck out."

"Of my own place?"

"That's why I came looking for you." He walked behind her and wrapped his arms around her. He kissed the side of her neck and then stared at her painting. "You don't strike me as a nature artist."

"I use commission work like this to practice my skills." The lies came too easily. This was why they had to be casual. She'd hate herself if she had to lie to someone she loved.

Love? What the hell, brain?

"Going to be working long?" he asked.

"Not sure."

"Want me to go?"

She should say yes. Make a point of this being casual. But instead, she said, "You can stay. There's an open bottle of wine on the counter if you want some."

He kissed her neck again and flexed his fingers around her before letting her go. He went to the counter and picked up the wine. "Glass?"

"Coffee cups next to the sink."

He chuckled.

"Are you making fun of my fine stemware?"

He turned with a mug in his hand. "I'm no etiquette expert, but I'm pretty sure it needs to have a stem to be called stemware."

"Just be glad I'm willing to share my cheap wine with you."

"No wine glass *and* the alcohol is cheap?"

She laughed. "What'd you expect for a late-night hookup? I already got mine. It's not like I have to impress you now."

"Funny." He poured himself some wine and then sat on the floor next to her while she painted.

"There is a couch over there. I'm sure you'd find it more comfortable than the floor."

"But that's pretty far away, and I wouldn't be able to do this from over there." His hand wrapped around her ankle and then up the inside of her leg.

She instinctively clenched her thighs as warmth pooled low in her belly. His hand stopped just above her knee.

"I thought you were painting."

She realized that at his touch, she froze, palette knife in hand. Shaking off the sensations, she said, "You distracted me."

Refocusing on the canvas, she smeared the dark green on as part of a tree.

"Hmm," he hummed from the floor. "I like watching you work."

She did her best to ignore him, but then his hand continued north and her eyes fluttered closed as the possibility of pleasure washed over her.

"Do you want me to stop?"

She shook her head. When she opened her eyes, he was kneeling in front of her.

"Was that a no, don't stop?"

"Definitely don't stop." She set the knife on the table.

As he rose from his place on the floor, he scooped her up. She wrapped her legs around him. His fingers cradled her bare ass and he groaned upon finding she wore nothing under the T-shirt. He carried her up the stairs like that, caressing her while she kissed him. London had never been drawn to big, burly guys but she definitely saw the appeal right now.

A girl could get used to being the total focal point of a man's desire. It was like he couldn't get enough of her and her body became his plaything, for both their pleasure.

Ezra woke in the morning and London was gone again. Didn't the woman sleep? He sat up and gathered his clothes from where they'd been tossed the night before. He got dressed and went downstairs. On his way, he smelled coffee, the scent drawing him to the small kitchen area.

"Hey," London said. "I was just about to wake you. I have some stuff I need to do today, and I have to get going soon."

"No problem. I'm sure if I don't get to the shop soon, Bronte will be calling."

"No rush. You can have some coffee first."

He walked close, took her cup from her hand, and took a drink. It was too sweet, like her. He couldn't stop the grimace.

"I wasn't offering you my coffee. It's not for everyone."

"With that much sugar, it's no surprise you barely sleep." He reached around her for a new mug and poured half a cup for himself. Black.

"I sleep. It's just a slightly unconventional schedule."

"Hmm-mm." He gulped his coffee so he could get out of her way. He didn't want to overstay his welcome because he wanted to be invited back. "Can I see you again?"

"You'll see me tomorrow when I come by to pick up my stuff."

"Or I could deliver it."

"Mr. Fisher, are you trying to get invited back into my bed?"

"In your bed, your house...you." The thought had him hardening in his jeans. He leaned over and kissed her cheek. She shivered at the slight touch, and he was sure she was remembering all the places his lips had traveled last night.

She released a shuddering breath. "That is quite the offer."

He kept his face close to hers and stared into her bright blue eyes. "That wasn't a yes."

She blinked quickly. "Yes, please deliver my items to me. I might even get some better wine for you."

"No need. You're more than enough to satisfy me." He kissed her neck to feel the rapid pulse there. Then he pulled away, and said, "Call me later."

Her eyes had drifted closed like they had at his touch last night. When they opened and she smiled up at him, he wanted to stay and take her back to bed. That look she gave him, while heated, reflected more than just wanting to fuck. He wanted more of her.

He just hoped he'd have a chance. As his car warmed up, he checked his phone. Sure enough, he'd missed a text from his sister. Rather than explain anything, he simply texted that he'd had a late night but would be in soon.

The drive home was fast, as traffic was light for a late Sunday morning. He showered quickly and by the time he got to the shop, Bronte was antsy.

"What's going on?" he asked.

"You tell me."

"I don't know what you're talking about."

"Oh my God. Really?" She huffed. "You and London. She was the reason for your late night, right?"

"Yeah." He moved through the studio and hoped Bronte still had coffee.

"Yeah what?" she called after him.

"Yeah, I was with London."

"And?" His sister practically vibrated with excitement.

He was tired and severely undercaffeinated and had no energy to deal with that. "We fucked every which way and both left satisfied."

"Ew. I was not looking for that kind of detail."

"You shouldn't be looking for any kind of detail. Stay out of it." He drank his coffee and went to the pile of orders he had on his desk.

"The window looks nice. I hope you at least told her she did a good job."

He grunted his response. Had he told her? He'd thanked her, right? Now his stupid sister had him questioning his every move. He thumbed through the orders and checked promised-by dates. Of course, everyone wanted their one-of-a-kind Christmas gifts before the holiday, so his next week would be slammed to allow time for fuckups.

At least it would keep his mind off London. He hoped.

"In the very good news department, I got a slew of people interested in taking classes. If we make this a regular thing, it'll be a nice bump in revenue."

"Uh-huh." He was already at his table planning the glass set he needed to make.

"Was that you agreeing, or you telling me to shut up?"

"Both."

She rounded the table and stood in his path to the glass. He huffed.

"I'm really having a hard time reading you right now. You're acting all grumpy. Like grumpier than normal, but you just agreed to let me hold more classes without even so much as a growl about people invading your space." She tilted her head in examining him. "I like the effect she has on you. I hope she sticks around."

"Not likely."

"Oh, man. Did you already scare her off?"

"Not that it's your business, but no. We're just casual."

Bronte smirked and stepped away. "If she was just casual for you, I would never know about it."

Then she turned and walked away. He got to work, shoving away thoughts of Bronte and everything she'd said about London. She only knew about London because she'd specifically asked. Otherwise, she would have no idea.

But he had to admit, in the quiet space of his own mind that the last few days with London did make him feel different. The quiet of the shop felt different. He'd quickly become accustomed to her singing and dancing, cursing when things went wrong.

It wasn't until hours later that he remembered that he did in fact sign on for Bronte to do more classes. London had fucked with his brain more than he'd thought.

Chapter Thirteen

Ezra had done well for the past day and a half. He hadn't called London at all, even though he'd wanted to just show up at her place. He might not be the smartest man alive but even he knew that showing up uninvited wasn't a good way to keep a woman's interest. She'd texted him last night when he was already in bed and they chatted via text for a while, talking about the projects they'd been working on.

Tonight, they had tentative plans for him to come by with her tree toppers. Part of him wished that they broke while in the annealer because then she'd be forced to come back to the studio to make more. But he wasn't that much of a dick.

He barely saw Bronte all day. She'd been busy in the shop and talking to people about scheduling her next class. When it was time to grab London's tree toppers, he got suddenly nervous. He wanted them to be good for her.

Standing in front of the annealer, he hesitated to open it. She'd made three. Surely at least one would be okay. He'd never had every product he made break.

"You might as well get it over with."

He looked over his shoulder at his sister.

"If they're all crap, you can bring her flowers to cheer her up."

He shook his head. "I think she'd prefer a bottle of wine."

Without waiting for Bronte's snarky comment, he swung open the door. As he grabbed the first topper, he saw that the top half listed to the side. "Fuck."

Setting that one on the table, he reached for the second one, but he didn't have to touch it to know that it was broken. There was a split down the side. He took a deep breath and reached for the third. Carefully pulling it out, he inspected it. It was in one piece and it was straight. He turned it in his hands and found no cracks.

He turned to show Bronte, but she was beside him with a padded box for him to set it in.

"She really did it, huh?"

"Looks like it."

"You heading out now?"

"No. I have a few more things to wrap up here. You can head out if you want. Just lock up the front."

"Okay. Let me know if you need me to cover tomorrow. You know, if you're too busy or tired from celebrating." She winked and walked away.

He put the box on his desk and went to finish the vase he was making for another commission. He worked fast but not carefully, and it came out a little misshapen. London on the brain was not good for his work ethic.

He decided to take a quick break, have some water, and reset his brain. Sitting on his stool, he took out his phone and scrolled through social media and the news. An article popped up that caught his attention.

It wasn't so much the article as the image attached to it. A red piece of glass that was shaped eerily like the one he had sitting in a box in his office. He opened the article.

CHICAGO BUSINESSMAN TO AUCTION ONE-OF-A-KIND MAXWELL TREE TOPPER

The headline set off sirens in his head. When he'd seen London's sketches, he'd had a nagging feeling of familiarity but he couldn't place it. Now he couldn't escape it. His father had taught him about this piece. The fame it had brought Maxwell drove him into isolation.

Why would London want to imitate this?

Could her mother have a thing for a Maxwell imitation? Possibly, but not likely. From the very beginning when London had told him about her proposition, he'd had an uneasy feeling but ignored it.

What the fuck was she up to?

He began replaying conversations they'd had. Then he remembered her notebook and how she'd been sketching famous art. And the one in her studio she was working on the other night, saying it was a commission to work on her skills.

Skills, my ass. She's a forger.

The thought came on so quickly and so strongly, he knew it was right.

"Fuck me," he said to the empty studio. Rage filled him and he wanted to smash something. He thought of the tree topper. He could break it and tell her that none of them came out.

But then, he'd be no better than her lying ass. No. He deserved the truth, so he'd confront her.

He grabbed his keys and the topper and headed to her house. In his car, he texted her. On my way. We need to talk.

As he started the engine, she responded. That doesn't sound good. Is everything ok?

No, it fucking was not okay. Rather than answer her, he just took off out of the lot. On the entire trip, he tried to convince himself that there could be a million other reasons for her to be copying art. Maybe it really was practice.

Then why say she'd been commissioned?

His brain spun in circles. He wanted to believe she was innocent of the thought he was having, but that didn't make it so. He shouldn't care.

Maybe he could just walk away without confronting her, but by using his studio—using *him*—he was part of whatever shit she was into. And it pissed him off.

He whipped into the visitor spot, grabbed the box, and stormed to the door. He jabbed at the bell. Less than a minute later, the door swung open and London stood there with a huge smile on her face. She looked genuinely happy to see him.

"You made great time. Come on in. It's cold out there."

He realized that he was just staring at her and not moving.

Stepping into the building, he said, "What are you up to?"

She glanced over her shoulder. "What do you mean?"

"I mean, who the fuck are you trying to fool with this forgery?"

There was a hitch in her stride and she turned to face him, halfway to her door. "What are you talking about? I told you I was copying the style for a gift."

He gritted his teeth and shoved the box at her so he could pull out his phone. As he opened the article, she said, "Come inside and tell me what has you so mad."

He followed her into her loft and without closing the door, he thrust his phone in her face. "This."

She focused on the words and paled. Setting the box down on the floor, she took the phone from him and began scrolling.

"Now tell me how it's *not* a forgery."

Clutching his phone, she said, "It's not what you think."

"Yeah, what is it?"

She licked her lips and took a deep breath.

"Need some time to get your lie together?"

"I haven't—"

He stared at her, waiting for the next lie to come.

"Okay." She handed him his phone. "I

haven't been totally honest. The topper is not a gift for my mother."

"Surprise."

"But it's not what you think."

"What do I think? That you used me and my studio to create a forgery that you hope to pass off as the original?"

Her hands curled into fists. "Look. I can't tell you everything because there are other people involved and I can't risk them. I wasn't totally honest about the topper, but everything else we talked about was me. What happened between us was real. I like you. But this other stuff is why I'm not in a position to be in a relationship."

"How real is anything with you? Your studio is full of forgeries." He pointed at the canvases in the corner.

"Yes. But there's a good reason for it." She took another breath and wrapped her arms around her middle. "Without going into detail...remember when we talked about what happened to your dad and I asked if you would ever want to get revenge on the guys who scammed him? That's what I'm doing."

He huffed. Each lie was more outrageous than the last. "You want me to believe you're some kind of fucking Robin Hood?"

"Kind of."

"Robin Hood was a thief. But at least he took care of those around him. He didn't put people at risk unknowingly. You used me and my studio for your shit."

"This will never come back on you. Please."

She reached out to touch him and he jerked back. "I wouldn't do that."

"Did you choose me intentionally, or was it luck of the draw?"

"What do you mean?"

He stood closer and stared into her eyes. "Did you target me because of my father?"

"Originally, my friend reached out to you, but I didn't know that. I really did choose your studio because Bronte was offering a class. I thought I could get the basics and figure out how to make what I needed. I never expected to like you and want to spend time with you."

"I can't believe anything that comes out of your mouth." He vibrated with rage. And hurt. "At least the guys who fucked over my father did it legally. They were unethical and immoral, but he chose to work with them. You're the illegal version of them. And you made me an unwitting partner in your crime. You duped me into letting you in, and that's worse than all the rest."

"Ezra, please—"

"Take your fucking topper and do whatever you want. Don't ever darken my door again." He kicked the box, sending it sliding across the floor until it smacked into the table leg. He turned and stormed out.

LONDON STOOD FROZEN IN SHOCK FOR A FEW minutes, staring at her open door. It wasn't until a tear plopped on her shirt that she realized she was crying. So many thoughts swirled in her head. She had a topper—maybe, if it hadn't broken—but Bruce Moore was advertising that he was auctioning the topper. She swiped at her tears. She needed to get to Audrey and Nikki in case they didn't already know.

She sent them a text with 911. After locking the door, she looked at the box on the floor. She needed to know if the topper was salvageable, but she couldn't force herself to do it yet. With the topper being in the press, it might not even matter. Their entire job might be blown out of the water.

While waiting for the girls to show up, she opened a new bottle of wine and poured a huge mug. Even as she did, she was reminded of Ezra's teasing about her lack of stemware.

Fuck. They'd only spent one night together. He shouldn't have this kind of effect on her. Sipping her wine, she sat on the couch and took a mental inventory of the progress she'd made on the other pieces. Every other thought she had was of Ezra, though. Maybe she should've just gone to the apartment and asked Audrey and Nikki to meet her there instead of at her place.

A few months ago, that would've been automatic. But now, Audrey was at Jared's and Nikki at Wade's, so the home base was just being used for work. The girls weren't living there anymore. But she could sit there and not have any reminders of Ezra.

Her bell rang and she went to let Nikki and

Audrey in. "Sorry to call you both here when I'm sure you were hanging with your guys."

"No worries. We were actually just leaving the apartment when you called, so we had Jared's driver bring us here," Audrey said. "What's wrong?"

She waved for them to follow her into her place.

Behind her, Nikki said, "This can't be good. Did the topper not work?"

London shrugged. She still hadn't opened the box.

"Was hot glass guy a dud in the sack?"

"Nikki!" Audrey admonished as she closed and locked the loft door.

"What? I'm just sayin' that would be a hell of a letdown."

London blew out a long deep breath. "The topper is in that box. Not sure if it's still in one piece. I haven't had the courage to look. Ezra delivered it tonight, along with a fat stack of accusations about me being a forger."

"What?" Audrey asked, at the same time Nikki said, "Fuck me."

London set her wine on the table and picked up her tablet. "I don't know how or why he came across this, but he showed me this article." She turned her tablet for them to see.

Nikki was already across the room pouring wine for her and Audrey.

Audrey said, "Yeah, that's why we were at the apartment. We were digging to find out when the auction is happening and trying to see if the insurance company has already appraised it."

"What do we do now?" London asked.

"First, sit down and tell us what happened with Ezra." Audrey pulled her toward the couch where Nikki refilled her wine.

"I don't think we have to worry about him telling anyone. He was mad and all, but mostly he was hurt that I lied to him and used him."

"I'm not asking in we're in danger. We're good at covering our tracks. I mean, what happened with the two of you?"

London curled up in the corner of the couch. "Doesn't matter now. He'll never speak to me again." She shook her head. "He wouldn't let explain. Not that I could say much, but I could tell that it didn't matter what came out of my mouth. He wasn't going to listen."

"Then he's a dick," Nikki said, plopping on the other end of the couch.

"Shh," Audrey said. "London is really upset."

"As she should be. If he won't even listen..."

"I really like him. More than I probably should."

"Would it help if you explained to him what we're doing?" Audrey asked.

"What?" Nikki yelled. "Give some rando the power to put us all away? What are you smoking?"

"You told Wade everything and trusted him."

"But he's Wade. We have history and his is far from clean."

"And what about his partners? Isn't one of them an ex-cop? He told them, and yet, we're still here."

"He didn't tell them everything."

London raised a hand. "You can stop fighting. It doesn't matter. I tried to tell him that I'm not some forger looking for a quick buck. That we're trying to get revenge on the rich assholes who take advantage of people."

"And that wasn't good enough for him?" Nikki scoffed.

"He questioned my ability to be like Robin Hood because I put him at risk by using him."

"We wouldn't let anything happen to him," Audrey said.

"I know. But he doesn't." She sighed. "Like I said. It doesn't matter. We just need to come up with a plan."

"Well, if none of your toppers worked, Moore gets away with his millions," Nikki said.

"Or he'll pass them on to Jared and Mia's dads," Audrey added.

London waved a hand in the direction of the box. "The last one is in the box. I was too afraid to open it."

Nikki jumped up and grabbed the box. She gave it a little shake. "Not shattered," she said with a smile. Then, she flipped up the lid.

After moving some paper aside, she winced.

"Fuck," London said.

"It's not totally destroyed." Nikki pulled out a piece of the topper. The tip of the spire had broken off. "I say we try super glue."

"I agree," Audrey said.

"Really?" Nikki questioned. "You never agree with me."

"As long as it's good enough to fool Moore and his guests while it's on the tree, that's all we need. An obvious imperfection will never pass authentication."

"I don't know," London said.

"Slap some fake diamonds on that puppy and we're good." Nikki settled the topper back in the box.

London shot her friends a skeptical look.

"Audrey already found that the insurance company is going to authenticate after the party, so we're still on for stealing it. How fast can you make this work?"

"I'll have it ready. I have nothing to occupy myself, so I'll make sure it's done. The Taggert painting is halfway done too, so plan that one."

Nikki smiled. "I guess a little heartbreak is good motivation for work, huh?"

"You would know," Audrey said.

"This isn't the same," London replied. "Me and Ezra..." She lifted a shoulder.

Audrey touched her arm. "I'm no expert on people—"

Nikki snorted.

With a roll of her eyes, Audrey continued, "This thing with Ezra might not've been love, but you shouldn't treat it like it's nothing, either."

"Tomorrow, glue and fake diamonds. Tonight, all the wine," Nikki said and refilled their mugs.

London suddenly realized that she kept telling herself she was an outsider in this group, but she'd been wrong. These women had become family.

Chapter Fourteen

London woke with blurry eyes and a fuzzy mouth. She stumbled off her couch and saw a note from Audrey sitting on the table.

Take the pills. Drink the water. Let us know if you need help with your project.

Project. The damn diamonds on the tree topper. She swallowed the ibuprofen sitting on a plate and took a swig of water. She started a pot of coffee and went to take a shower while it brewed. Today was a new day. Ezra Fisher would not be taking up space in her brain.

As the hot water beat down on her thumping head, she developed her game plan. She would just pretend that her fling with Ezra came to its natural end. A casual thing had an expiration date. She just had to ignore the memory of the pain on his face when he'd called her a liar.

After her shower and a full cup of coffee, she was ready to get to work. She set the broken topper on her work table and pulled out the zirconia that Jared procured. She glued the tip back on the topper and let it set. While it dried, she reviewed the sketch she made of how to apply the diamonds. They swirled on an angle so she needed to line out where to go.

With a white marker, she laid out some lines and prayed the lines would be hidden by the gems. She started with a short line of glue and pressed a gem onto it with a pair of tweezers. Then she went on to the next and the next.

As tedious as she thought glassblowing was, this was worse. She turned the glass in her hand to decide the best path to take. The act of turning the topper made her think of Ezra.

His big hands covering hers to guide the glass and tubing. Cracking jokes with him about applying pressure. The feel of his hands on her skin.

She jolted with the memory. No. She had to stop. Audrey and Nikki needed her to focus. She laid out the next line of glue and pressed more gems into place. She forced other topics into her head. Mia had told her to reach out to some galleries to see about creating her own show. What if she did an entire show of forgeries? That would certainly be a commentary on the value of originality in society.

The ridiculous thought had her smiling. If Ezra wasn't so pissed at her, he probably would've laughed since everything he made was unique.

More memories of Ezra swamped her. In only a few short days, she'd become accustomed to his grumpy nature and had even grown kind of fond of it. His grumpiness hadn't been mean or angry. He was a bit of a perfectionist and having people mess with his routine or space didn't sit well with him.

She could relate to that. Laying the gems on the topper started to go a little faster as she got a rhythm going. She worked all day and into the evening—despite the nagging hangover—until her eyes were bleary and her fingers cramped.

While she'd taken breaks to stretch and jump around, she'd begun to feel a little hunchbacked. Coffee was no longer working to keep her focused.

She studied the red glass in her hand. The fake diamonds glinted in the light.

Was Ezra right? Was she worse than the men they were targeting?

She never would've let anything blow back on him. Until last night, he'd had plausible deniability. He'd done nothing wrong. He worked with a paying customer. Yeah, that's all she was supposed to be.

Her eyelids started to droop, so she set the topper down to finish drying before tackling the other side.

A quick nap and she could get back at it. She couldn't let the team down. She set an alarm for an hour on her phone, folded her arms on the workbench, and lay her head down.

Sleep fell over her quickly, but dreams of Ezra plagued her.

In that light, sleepy dream, she was entranced by his gentle smile, the roped muscles of his forearms, the bulk of his chest. She reached for his talented hands to pull him close.

The loud blaring of the alarm jolted her awake, pulling her from Ezra once again. With her eyes still mostly closed, she reached out to turn off the horrible ringing.

In her fumbling, a nagging thought poked the back of her mind. But she continued to stretch out her arm.

Then suddenly she was wide awake and conscious of the fact that she'd bumped the topper. Everything moved in slow motion. She saw it doing a wobbly roll off the edge of the table but she couldn't grab it.

She practically leaped onto the workbench to catch it, but she didn't move fast enough. As she lay sprawled over the table, fake diamonds scattered under her, digging into her skin, the topper fell to the floor and broke.

London stared at it for a full minute unable to comprehend what she'd done.

Then she scrambled off the table and around to the other side. She carefully lifted pieces.

"Shit. This thing is cursed." She mentally berated herself for not securing the topper better, for not just going up to bed, and for screwing up everything with Ezra.

After setting all the pieces back on the table, she made a fresh pot of coffee. "No sleep for the wicked. Karma is a bitch."

She spent hours gluing the topper back together, but every time she had a good portion together, another piece fell off. She couldn't figure out if the glue wasn't working or if the damn thing was really cursed.

By three am, she gave up. She had tiny cuts all over her fingers from the glass, but the glue was at least keeping them from bleeding everywhere. Nothing was working. She was a total failure. She let the team down, not to mention all the people who would've been helped by the sale of this thing.

She snapped a picture of the pile of glass and sent a text to Nikki and Audrey. I failed.

Then she opened a new bottle of wine, sat on the couch, and cried.

"WHAT KIND OF FUCKED UP MESS IS THIS?"

London popped one eye open to find Nikki staring down at her. "What are you doing here?"

"Had a feeling you were a mess."

London sat up and ran a hand over her face. "How did you get in here?"

Nikki shot her a disbelieving look. "Thief, remember?"

The bell rang and Nikki answered the door.

"How bad is it?" Audrey asked.

"Pretty bad." Nikki pointed at her. "Please tell me I never looked like that."

"Thanks, guys." London rolled her eyes, but the movement hurt too much, so she closed them again and lay back down.

She heard her friends moving around but

couldn't muster enough care to look to see what they were doing. Then she smelled coffee. Her stomach growled but the brew smelled good.

Cool fingers brushed her hair away from her face. "Go take a shower. You'll feel a little better," Audrey said.

"Ugh."

"She's being nice. You stink like a wino. Go take a shower so we can clean this up."

London forced herself off the couch. "You don't need to clean up. I'm fine."

"Sure," Nikki said.

She didn't have it in her to argue, so she went to shower. The hot water helped but she couldn't remember the last time she ate. Food would probably be better than coffee, but she really wanted the coffee.

When she got back downstairs, the empty wine bottle was gone, her dirty coffee mugs were clean, and there was a breakfast burrito waiting for her. "Damn, you guys work fast."

"Nikki had food ordered before we got here. And it looks like it was a smart move. You have nothing here but wine and coffee."

"I've been busy." London waved a hand and unwrapped her breakfast burrito.

"What's with the pity party?" Nikki said.

London swallowed her food and the fast-forming lump in her throat. "I worked all day and night last night on the topper. And I totally fucked it up. I was tired and couldn't focus." She shook her head and tugged at the sandwich wrapper. "I was caught up in my own thoughts about

Ezra, and…" She sighed and pointed to the workbench. "It's not fixable."

"Okay." Nikki gave her one of those so-the-fuck-what looks.

"I let you guys down. We can't do the Moore job. That would've been a ton of money to help people."

Audrey patted her leg. "Shit happens. We considered not doing this one anyway. No big deal. We have plenty of others."

"But we all wanted this one."

"Fuck it. We can get him some other way," Nikki said. "The topper was what Mia picked. I'm sure he has something else we can steal."

Her friends' acceptance of her screw-up didn't make her feel better. "Thanks," she said, half-heartedly.

"How much of this is about the topper and how much is about hot glass guy?"

Tears clawed at London as she looked at Nikki. "I don't even know anymore." She waved a hand. "And before you say anything else, I know how stupid it is. We barely know each other. I shouldn't be so caught up in it. Him. But there was something about the way he looked at me when he came here. I can't shake it."

"Have you tried talking to him again?" Audrey asked.

She shook her head. "He made it clear he *never* wants to hear from me again."

"Is there anything we can do to help?" Audrey offered.

"No. It's time to move on to the next job. I'm going to get back to work on the paintings as soon as I finish eating and get some more sleep. My brain is still too foggy to function and I'll be really pissed if I screw up another one."

"I say we go egg his shop," Nikki said.

"God, no. Leave the poor man alone. He didn't do anything."

Nikki rose, tossed her wrapper in the trash, and said, "He made you cry, babe, and that's enough in my book."

One thing she loved about Nikki was how loyal she was. If you had her in your corner, you were in good shape.

"As much as I appreciate that, Ezra was right. I did use him. I just never expected him to find out." She took a few more bites of her burrito. "Really. You guys can go."

"You sure?" Audrey asked.

"Yes, and I would appreciate it if you didn't break into my place again."

"I make no promises," Nikki called as she strode out the door.

Audrey laughed and gave her a hug. "Give us a call if you need anything."

"I will." She locked up behind them and crawled into bed, determined to not give Ezra any more space in her mind.

Ezra hadn't slept. He'd fucked up four different pieces he'd tried to complete for orders.

His bad mood was then compounded by his sister pestering him.

He felt her presence in the studio even though she hadn't said anything. He'd been pretty sure the last time he'd yelled at her would've been enough to keep her away. Apparently, he was wrong.

"What do you want, Bronte?"

"You got a package."

He looked over his shoulder where she held a large brown envelope. He didn't remember ordering anything that would show up in an envelope. Probably fancy junk mail. "Toss it on the desk."

"You sure?"

He glared at her.

She held up one hand while keeping the envelope pressed to her chest with the other. "It came via courier with no return address. It's either super fishy or super special."

Her statement had him thinking of London. Again. He'd had those suspicious feelings about her and he'd ignored them. He growled and then said, "Desk."

"Fine. Whatever. At some point, you need to talk about whatever has you so messed up. It's not healthy to keep it bottled up."

He knew she meant well, but he couldn't admit to her that he'd been as gullible as their father. At least he'd figured it out before he lost everything. His heart was a little dinged up, but he'd get over it. He turned back to the flames, and his sister went to the front of the store.

After managing to finally get a vase done to replace one that was purchased from the window display, Ezra felt a little better. His brain was coming back online and things would get back to normal.

He owed Bronte an apology for his excessive attitude, so he decided to buy her lunch. In his office, he called their favorite pizza place. After he placed his order, he looked at the envelope Bronte had left on his desk.

He picked it up. The handwriting was neat but nothing special. No return address as she'd said. He ripped open the flap and a file folder slipped out. A typed note was attached to the top:

You don't know me, but we have a mutual friend. She meant you no harm and what she said was the truth. Look through the folder and connect the dots yourself. The project created in your shop broke and she has no way to replace it, so you no longer have to worry about being attached to it.

What the fuck was London doing now? He sat down and opened the folder. Inside he found a set of articles about recent forgeries. He'd been right. Part of him wished he was wrong and he'd overreacted. This was proof that she was a forger.

He was about to toss it on the desk and get back to work when another list caught his eye. It was a simple spreadsheet with names and amounts. The title of the page was Victims of Benson and Towers.

Those names hit him hard. He knew his father's losses were nowhere near as bad as others suffered. They were helping those victims? It explained a lot—why London had asked so many questions about his father, why she showed up at his studio.

He rubbed his beard and went back to the top of the pile and read the articles. By the time the pizza arrived, he was thoroughly confused. If he connected the dots correctly, it seemed that London was creating forgeries and selling the originals to give the money to victims of the Benson and Towers scam. There was no way she could be doing it all herself. Was there really a friend who sent him this information? And why?

"You opened it!" Bronte screeched from behind him with the pizza in hand. "What is it?"

He quickly folded everything back into the folder.

"Seriously? You bribe me with pizza for lunch and then you won't tell me what was delivered via *courier*? Like that's not suspicious."

He blew out a long breath. This was Bronte. He could trust her. And she wasn't likely to drop it anyway. Pulling out his phone, he said, "The other night, I found this article."

He handed her the phone showing the article about the tree topper going up for auction.

"That's London's thing."

"Yeah. So I confronted her about forging a copy. I didn't know what her plan was, but I knew it was something shady. When I saw this, it pissed me off. She used me. Lied about what she was doing..."

Bronte flipped the lid on the pizza box and took a slice. "Well, in her defense, it's not like she could come in and say, 'Hey, I want to forge some priceless piece of glass.' She did say she was making a replica."

"For her mom. Another lie." He shook his head. "When we were stuck here during the snowstorm, I saw her sketchpad with some copies of famous paintings. She said she used them for practice. Then, at her place, she was painting a copy and mentioned it was a commission. This article was what put it together for me."

"Intriguing," she said around a mouthful of pizza. "What did she say when you confronted her? And what does that have to do with your mysterious package?"

"She claimed to be some kind of Robin Hood, said she was going after scammers. I didn't believe her." He slid the folder over to his sister. "Then this showed up."

Bronte wiped off her hands and opened the folder. Ezra sat back and ate some pizza while watching his sister's reactions as she read. She didn't speak, but her face said a lot.

"So?" she asked.

"So what?"

"What are you going to do? You were a total asshole and she's not the bad guy here."

He narrowed his eyes. "I think by definition, a criminal is a bad guy."

"Shut up. That's like saying someone who kills in self-defense is a murderer. It's not the same. Based on what this says, she's not doing it for self-profit. Maybe you should hear her out."

"To what end?"

"I can tell you like her. And if what this says is true—and really, why would anyone go to these lengths to sell this—that topper is worth more than a lot of these other forgeries. Think of the good she can do."

He should've known that his sister would've ended up in the same place he had. London had shown no qualms about throwing a ton of money at them for studio time. The spreadsheet showed college tuition paid for, and medical bills covered —it was a lot of good.

Even if they never had a chance as anything more than a one-night stand, he could help make a difference in the lives of others. He grabbed another slice of pizza and stood. "Fine. You win. I'll make her another topper."

"Really? And are you going to deliver it with a big side of *I'm an ass*? Or do you have a huge romantic gesture planned?"

"Shut the hell up. I don't have anything to apologize for. I was right."

Bronte helped herself to another slice. As she danced out of the office, she sang out, "But you want her back because she likes your grumpy ass."

Ezra grunted and rolled up his sleeves. London had wanted the topper done before this weekend, so if he started now, he could get it done. He didn't know what had happened to the last one, but ever since he'd looked at the stress fractures of the ones that didn't make it, he'd thought about how to change things to make it work.

He pulled an image up of the topper on his phone, but once he started working, he discovered that he didn't need it. Working on the topper, he heard every comment London had made about the dimensions and the color. As he worked, he made the glass a little thinner than she had, hoping for fewer issues with stress fractures. About halfway through, Bronte came back.

"Damn, you're fast. I told you that you should've helped her. It would've been a totally different situation."

And if he had, it might've been done right the first time, and he never would've had so much time with her.

"How are you going to keep it from breaking like all the others?"

"I'm thinking about doing some hand annealing before putting it in the annealer. And I've made the glass a little thinner but not too noticeable, I think."

He came around the table and studied the partially finished topper.

"Looks good to me. Do you want me to call her?"

"No. I'm just going to do this and have it delivered."

"What? You can't do that."

"Why not?" He turned back to reheat the glass before twisting the spire.

"After all this, you're just gonna walk away from someone you really like and who for some unfathomable reason is willing to put up with you and your cranky attitude? You're hopeless!" She flopped her arms around and stomped back to the front.

He knew he was hopeless which was why he was just going to give her this topper, assuming he could get it to work. What chance could they have? She was a forger. He wasn't even sure if she was a legitimate working artist or if this was it for her.

He didn't think he could live his life worrying about what she was doing and if she'd get caught. Since he couldn't control any of that, he focused on what he could do—make the best damn tree topper possible.

Chapter Fifteen

*L*ondon was covered in paint spatter. She'd been hopping from one painting to the next, sketching in between researching the artists and their methods. She'd thrown herself completely into her work. In the bit of downtime she took, she began planning a series she could pitch to the galleries Mia had put her in touch with. Overall, she was feeling pretty good and productive.

Except for the ache in her heart over Ezra.

She wished she had a way to make it up to him. The lies she told were more for his benefit than hers, but she doubted he'd see it that way.

Maybe she wasn't able to be with anyone until this job was over. Unless she found a criminal who wouldn't mind what she was involved in. How did one go about meeting a like-minded criminal? Was there a dating app for that?

She laughed at the ridiculous turn her thoughts had taken. At least she wasn't feeling quite as mopey.

When her bell rang, she sighed. She told Audrey and Nikki she was fine and was busy working. They didn't need to keep checking on her.

She tromped to the door and opened it, saying, "I told you I'm fine."

But she pulled up short when she realized it wasn't her friends. A delivery guy was staring at her.

"I'm glad you're fine. London?"

"Yes. Please step in out of the cold."

He crossed the threshold and handed her a package and a small screen. "I have a package for you. Please sign here."

She signed with her finger and locked him out. On the way back into her loft, she shook the box. Inside, she slid a knife under the edge and lifted the lid. A note on top was written in a pretty script, and she almost fell over when she saw the signature. Ezra.

SHE STUDIED THE CURVES OF THE WRITING. The man continued to surprise her in unusual ways. He had pretty handwriting. If she had to guess she would've thought he wrote in chicken scratch or heavy block letters.

She moved the paper aside and found a new topper. How the hell? It was beautiful in a way none of hers had been. She lifted it carefully from the package. It was lighter than the ones she made. Why did he do this?

She called Audrey and put the phone on speaker while she set up to add the diamonds to the topper.

"Hey, what's up?" Audrey said.

"You're never going to believe what was just delivered."

"A stripper gram?" Nikki yelled in the background.

"A new tree topper. And it's perfect. Ezra sent it with a note saying I gave him ample evidence. What the hell is going on?"

Audrey sighed. "I sent him a little package the other day. Much like Mia did when she wanted to prove that we're doing good here. Nothing that would be considered legal evidence, but enough to make him believe you."

"Why would you take that risk?"

"You're worth it. You were hurting. I didn't ask him to make a new topper. In fact, I pointed out that the one you made broke, so he would have no connection to anything."

"And yet, he made me a new one." London tried to let that sink in. What did that mean? "Well, needless to say, we're back on for this heist."

"Woo-hoo!" Nikki called. "Keep Friday night free. We're going in."

London stared at the topper. It only gave her a couple of days to get all the diamonds on. "When's the party?"

"Saturday."

"Cutting it close."

"Keeps things interesting."

"Audrey?"

"I'm still here. Just digging through Moore's security."

"Do you think you can get me on the invite list for the party? With a plus-one."

"Oh, you dirty girl. You want to see your forgery in action, don't you?"

London smiled. "I want Ezra to see. If I can convince him to come."

"It'll be black tie."

"I know." Wheels started turning. She'd enlist Bronte's help. But first, diamonds.

FRIDAY CAME UP FAST. SHE DROVE TO THE apartment to meet Audrey and Nikki with the topper packed in a box and strapped into the passenger seat. She was not taking any more chances. It was a damn near-perfect replica.

When she pulled up outside the apartment, she texted Audrey to let her know. A minute later, Audrey was sliding into the back of the van with her tech bag. Nikki opened the passenger side door and unbuckled the seatbelt holding the box.

"You sure you want to do that?"

"It'll be fine." She climbed up and put the box in her lap. She opened it to look at the final product. "Wow. If I didn't know it was a fake..."

Audrey leaned forward between the seats. "Wow is right."

"It helps that a master glassblower made it and Jared got such high-quality gems."

"Stop dismissing your work." Nikki closed the lid. "We couldn't do this without you. Now, onto important stuff. Where are we eating?"

London laughed as she pulled out into traffic. Nikki always wanted some bad fast food right before a job. "Whatever you want."

"Chili dog and cheese fries, it is," Nikki said with a clap.

They hit a drive-through and parked to eat.

"What's the plan for this?" London asked as she ate a fry. "I feel a little out of the loop since I spent the last few days finishing the topper."

Audrey tapped on her laptop. "Once I disable the alarm, Nikki is going to do her favorite thing, scale a wall to get to the balcony on the second floor and use the patio door to get inside."

"I don't know that scaling the wall is my favorite thing. Rappelling down is way more fun."

Audrey rolled her eyes. "From the second floor, she'll rig herself to the rail and lower herself to make the swap."

"Easy-peasy." Nikki finished her chili dog and crumpled the wrapper.

To London, nothing Nikki did was easy.

"The Moores have left for an evening at the theater," Nikki said with a fake British accent. "So no one should be home."

"Sounds like you know what you're doing, as usual. Does Jared have a buyer for this?"

"Auction goes live tonight. We wanted to build the hype since this is such a special piece. The criminal underworld is buzzing about this."

London pulled out of the parking lot and headed to the Winnetka house of their target. The roads were clear but still slick as the Chicago weather fluctuated between a balmy 40 degrees during the day to 20 at night. London took Lake

Shore Drive north. The lake was dark and the beaches empty as the wind kicked up some pretty high waves.

She followed the GPS on her phone until they were winding through the streets of a sleepy little suburb of rich people. Although her parents were wealthy, she'd never spent time in the north shore suburbs that she'd been going to for the heists. Her parents toyed briefly with the idea of moving to the suburbs, but they opted to remain in the city.

With every trip out to the suburbs, she was grateful for her parents' decision. The suburbs were quaint and quiet, but she much preferred the noise and chaos of the city. She turned down the street where the Moores lived and slowed to a crawl. Cars in this neighborhood were parked safely in garages or driveways. Their black van stuck out, so she wouldn't be able to park and go unnoticed.

She drove past the house so Nikki could scope it out. Then she drove around the corner. "Where do you want me to drop you?"

Nikki was checking her backpack to make sure she had all of her tools. "Uh, pull over here and I'll jump out."

She checked her comms and got out of the vehicle as soon as London slowed to a stop.

"Catch you on the other side," Nikki said as she pulled her black knit hat over her head.

London pulled away. "At least wearing a hat isn't suspicious now that it's cold out. That would've been something for her to explain back in July."

"I'm sure she has a whole book of stories to explain away things."

"You know it," Nikki said in their ears.

"Turn here," Audrey said. "I need to stay close enough to make sure I have control of the alarm system."

"You got it." London drove around the block, slowly but not too slow because someone might notice. The cold weather was good for keeping people inside and the street was far enough from the front windows that even if someone looked, they would just see a van.

"Ready?" Nikki asked.

"Thirty seconds," Audrey answered.

"I would love to see how she's doing this," London commented.

"Done," Audrey said and climbed into the front seat. "I can tap into the indoor cameras. There's gotta be one that will catch her."

"I'm not here for your entertainment."

"Who are you kidding? You love to be the star," Audrey said. "You're very entertaining."

Nikki didn't respond, probably because she was climbing a wall. London turned the next corner. "I'm through the door. I love it when people don't worry about locking upstairs doors."

"Pull over by those bushes," Audrey directed.

London left the car running but turned off the lights. If a cop rolled up, they would just claim to be lost.

"Here you go," Audrey said, turning her laptop so they could both see the screen.

A moment later, Nikki's skulky form shifted in the shadows. She hooked her rigging to the rail and tugged. Then, she smiled and gave the camera a thumbs-up before sliding over the side of the rail. Upside down.

"How the heck does she do that upside down?" London whispered to Audrey. She didn't want to break Nikki's focus.

It took less than two minutes for Nikki to swap out the tree toppers. She flipped herself upright, tucked the topper into the box, and climbed back up. She disappeared into the shadows on the second floor.

"Okay. Time to roll. Take a left out of the house so you're not going the same way. We'll meet you."

"Yep," Nikki acknowledged.

Audrey kept her focus on the exterior cameras to keep an eye on Nikki in case something went haywire. London coasted down the street and turned the lights back on when she got to the corner. Nikki emerged from the shadows beside some bushes.

Her sudden appearance startled London. "Shit. Where did she come from? I thought we were going to have to wait for her."

"You get used to it." Audrey climbed into the back as Nikki opened the passenger door.

"Get used to what?" Nikki asked as she sat down.

"You popping up unexpectedly and scaring the shit out of everyone."

"Tools of the trade." Nikki took off her hat and then shook out her limbs. "It was almost too easy. I don't trust it. Are we sure this is the real thing?"

"Don't curse us by saying stuff like that." Audrey tapped away to reset the alarms and remove any evidence of Nikki. "Why would you complain when things go smoothly? That's like telling an actor good luck before going on."

"Psh. I don't believe in that superstitious crap. Let's go celebrate. Champagne is chilled and waiting for us."

London drove back to the apartment. Jared was waiting for them.

"Check it out," Nikki said, opening the box.

London stared at the topper, hoping hers was good enough to pass.

As if reading her mind, Nikki said, "Don't worry. If I didn't have them both, I wouldn't have been able to tell the difference."

"Cool."

Jared poured champagne for all of them. "Congratulations on the best score yet. The auction is open and the bids are flying."

London felt better knowing how much good they could do with all of that money. She sat on the couch and stared at the topper still sitting in the box.

Audrey plopped next to her. "You're good for the party tomorrow. Jared and I are going, and Mia is supposed to be there with Logan."

"Are you coming, too?" London asked Nikki.

"Hell, no. Returning to the scene of the crime? Not my style. Unless I get to rub someone's face in my brilliance." She sighed. "But since Moore won't know yet that I got him, there's no fun in that."

"I don't know, it might be fun for all of us to

be there and know, even if he doesn't." She sipped her champagne. "Does Mia know we hit this one?"

Audrey eyed Jared. "She shouldn't. She's supposed to be out of everything. So, unless Jared said something."

"I did not."

"But she'll know if we're all there. Will Logan know?"

Audrey shrugged. "Maybe. Nothing to worry about, though."

"If you say so."

"Are you coming even if Ezra refuses?"

"I'm not sure. I want to see the fake topper on the tree, but if he won't see me..."

"If he won't see you, fuck him," Nikki said. "If he can't respect that we're doing the right thing, then he doesn't deserve you."

London knew Nikki made an excellent point, but it didn't make her feel better.

Chapter Sixteen

_E_zra couldn't believe he was hiding in his office. Bronte had been acting weird all day. She was like a ball of nervous energy, and it annoyed the fuck out of him. It reminded him of when they were kids and she did something wrong and was trying to hide it.

Her poker face sucked.

He'd racked his brain for hours trying to figure out what she was hiding. She was supposed to have another class booked for tonight, so sitting in his office was the safest place until he had to do his required demonstration.

Rather than come get him, she sent a text. We're ready for you.

Weird.

He opened his office door and the voices from across the shop rang familiar. London was here. Emotion balled up in his gut but he didn't know what it was. He froze in the doorway.

Anger.

Relief.

Happiness?

He strode down the hall, got to the studio, and crossed his arms. Her back was to him and she was wearing another completely inappropriate dress for glasswork. The back was open except for the skinny straps at her shoulders. The middle dipped into a deep vee that stopped at the top of her ass. The midnight-blue material clung to her curves, much like the gold dress had, which made him remember it pooled at her feet.

She giggled like she had the first day they met, and then she spun, showing off the dress. When her eyes met his she froze. Her smile faded.

He looked past her to his sister. "I thought you had a class."

Bronte pointed to London. "She's our class."

He huffed.

"She paid for six spots."

"She can't work like that."

"*She* is standing right here. And I don't plan to work. I booked the spots because then you couldn't slam the door in my face."

He raised his brows to let her know that yes, he could slam the door in her face if he wanted.

But he didn't want to.

"Refund her money."

"Look," London took a step closer with her hands up. "I just want to talk. Then, if you still want me to leave, I will, and I'll never bother you again."

She took a few more steps and her perfume wafted over to him, weakening his defenses.

"I know you're mad. And I get why. But since you made that topper for me, I figure you don't completely hate me." She reached out and touched his arm, her fingers cool on his skin.

"I think that's my cue to leave. I'm going out with friends, so if you need to use my apartment to freshen up, feel free," Bronte said, then disappeared through the front.

"Before I say anything else, I'm sorry. I'm sure you can figure out why I didn't tell you the truth, but more than wanting to keep my secret, I wanted to keep you safe. Until you figured it out because you saw the auction info, you had deniability."

"Is that what you tell yourself? You don't think the cops would show up here and take everything from me?"

"We wouldn't let that happen. And I know you don't have any reason to believe that, but it's true. We might not be on the right side of the law, but we're on the right side. Everything we do is to help people who have been taken advantage of and hurt—not cause more damage."

"Why me?"

"I didn't lie about that. I truly just found the online coupon promotion that Bronte ran. It wasn't until after I booked that I found out my colleague had called you. She reached out because she knew your father had been a victim."

He remembered the call and how he'd quickly shut her down. "So you targeted me."

"No." She shook her head. "My friend thought it was a two-for deal. We could pay you a lot of money to make amends to your family and get what we needed for our job. It wasn't about exposing you to danger or making you an accomplice."

Her fingers flexed on his arm. "And everything else between us was real. That was me. I never lied about who I am."

God help him, he wanted to believe her.

"Okay."

"Okay, what? You forgive me?"

"I suppose I do."

Her cheek twitched and he knew she was holding back a smile. "Then, I would like to invite you to a holiday party."

"What?"

"I know that we can't go back to how things were. But I'd like to give us a chance."

"Is this forgery thing your..." He couldn't think of what to call it. "Career?"

She stepped back and he missed her touch. "I'm an artist. This was a job that came to me because of those talents." She lifted her shoulders. "However, it wasn't the first time I'd used such talents. But, no, it's not my career. It is, however, an ongoing job. No, it's more of a mission."

"What happens if you get caught?"

"Well, I don't think we will. We're really good. Without going into too much detail, law enforcement was looking into some forgeries. Like the ones my friend sent you information about. But no one has tied anything to anyone specific. It looks as though all of these men who are friends with Benson and Towers—who benefited from that scam—furthered their shady business and tried to scam their insurance company or some unsuspecting buyer."

As she spoke, the pieces started to fall into place. While the information that they sent to him gave him an overview and showed him why they were doing it, now he understood what they were doing. It was actually kind of brilliant.

"Will you go with me to a party?"

He looked at her and then down at himself. "I'm not exactly dressed for a party like that."

"Bronte has a tux waiting for you upstairs."

He shook his head. He knew his sister was hiding something.

"Please come with me. And if you don't like what I show you, we'll walk away as friends. I won't bother you or convince your sister to interfere. I know not everyone would be comfortable with the life I live."

"So you want me to hang out in your life and see if it's for me?"

"I'm not everyone's cup of tea. I believe in full disclosure in a relationship." She flashed him a bright smile. "At least as much as I can reveal without exposing others."

He shouldn't care about a peek into her life. He didn't need the headache or drama she was sure to bring into his quiet life.

But he couldn't help but think that she was his cup of tea. He felt lighter with her than he had in ages. Checking out a party wasn't a commitment. She was giving him an out.

"It has to be a tux?"

"Sorry, but the party is black tie and if you walk in looking all angry and hot in your jeans and T-shirt, you'll definitely stand out."

"I'm supposed to trust my sister got a suit that fits?"

"I helped with that. I am a very good judge of size."

Her gaze raked over his body and it took all he had to not pull her into his arms and kiss her.

"You go change. I'll be in the car outside."

"We're taking your pedo van?"

She burst out laughing. "It's not a pedo van. And no, I have a rental car for the evening."

"I'll be out in a few minutes."

She picked up a coat from the stool and wrapped it around herself, covering up all her bare skin. At least he'd be able to focus a little better in the car if she was covered.

He watched her get behind the wheel as he locked up and went to his sister's apartment to change, questioning his sanity all the way.

London contained her composure until she got to the car and Ezra had gone upstairs. Then, she let loose with a shimmy and danced in the driver's seat. She'd gone into the studio hoping for Ezra's company tonight but not counting on it. The fact that he agreed to come to the party was a positive sign that she could repair the damage done.

They might have a chance at something after all.

She hadn't thought much about what that

meant. She went into this telling him she didn't want a relationship, but in the few days she'd been without him, she was lonely. Missing him shouldn't have been a thing. But it was.

So, she was taking notes from those around her and seeing where this might go. She turned on the radio and allowed the music to soothe her nerves. A little while later movement on the sidewalk caught her attention. Ezra locked up Bronte's door and turned.

Oh my freaking God. The man was sexy in a tux.

He was like a model for a big and tall men's shop. She never would've guessed that Bronte rented the damn thing. It fit him well.

He strode toward the car and opened the door. As he sat, she said, "You clean up good, Fisher."

"Not as good as you." He gave her a heated look as he buckled his seatbelt.

She pulled out and drove east.

"Are you going to tell me whose party we're going to? Where it is?"

"Nope. There's something I want to show you, and if I give you too many details, you might change your mind."

"Instead, you're holding me hostage in your car."

"If that's the way you choose to see it...however, I think it counts as consent since you willingly got into my car without the details."

"I'll keep that in mind next time you consent to something. I'm allowed to stretch that consent to suit what I want."

The low rumble of his voice and the promise of his words sent a shiver down her spine. *Next time.* There was definitely a crack in his resolve to stay mad at her.

She headed north again, taking nearly the same route she did last night, winding north into the quiet suburbs. Not that Ezra's studio was in a noisy suburb. It just felt busier than these wealthy suburbs with their huge trees and few street lights. It was so dark and quiet here.

"You're making me nervous here. Where are we going?"

She glanced at him. "You act like I just turned down an alley surrounded by abandoned buildings. No serial killer lair, I promise. It's a fancy holiday party. That's all."

He continued to scan the houses as they drove. As she neared the house, it was like pulling up on a winter wonderland. Lights were bright enough to see down the block. Decorations all the way down the driveway.

"That's where you're taking me?" he asked.

"Yep."

The circular drive in front of the house was full of cars, so people were parking on the street. London followed suit.

Enough people were being dropped off that parking wasn't intense—not like in the city. And since the snow from last week had mostly melted, the sidewalks were clear and dry. She found a spot about a block away, not that she could tell because blocks out here were not city blocks.

"Ready?" she asked as she turned off the ignition.

"Are you going to tell me why we're here?"

She smiled. "To have some excellent champagne, mingle among the upper crust, see how the worse half lives. It'll be interesting. Trust me."

"Those are dangerous words. They could get me in a lot of trouble."

"Not tonight. I promise."

They got out of the car and Ezra put his arm around her as they walked toward the house. At the door, they followed a small group and London glanced around to see if anyone was checking names against a list. Nothing. The Moores must've had more of an open-door policy than some of their friends. She slipped her coat off and found a line of coat racks in a closet, no one checking anything. *It's probably good that Nikki isn't here. This would be easy pickings.*

London picked up two flutes from a passing waiter and handed one to Ezra.

Two steps into the living room, Ezra froze. "What the fuck," he whispered and pulled her back.

Startled, she looked up at him. "What?"

"You brought me to the fucking house you plan to steal from?"

She smiled and patted his chest. "Nope. Take a look. A close look at *your* handiwork." She raised her brows, hoping he'd get it, and sipped her expensive champagne.

"Why are we here?"

She slipped her arm into the crook of his elbow and led him into the room. "I wanted you to see it. To know how well it turned out. And I want you to look around this room and these people and know that we don't feel an ounce of guilt about any of it."

"Your lack of guilt makes it okay?"

"Doing the right thing makes it okay. That one hunk of glass—as beautiful as it is—is going to help over a hundred people. People like your dad." She took his hand and gave it a little squeeze. "If we had been able to help him, he might not have sold the shop. You wouldn't have lost your legacy."

He looked over the crowd and then back at her. "All these people are bad?"

"No clue. But the host is not only good friends with Dwayne Benson and Cesar Towers, that piece of art on the tree is something he bought to hold money for them. Guys like him were funding the escape from U.S. law. We're just balancing the scales."

He didn't say anything else, but he also didn't pull away from her. She allowed her words to sink in. As she studied the guests, she saw Mia across the room. She briefly considered not talking to her, but she missed Mia.

Tugging Ezra's hand again, she said, "Come on. I see my friend. I want to introduce you."

"Friend? I thought you didn't like anyone here."

"I didn't say that. You're making assumptions." They crossed the room and she called, "Mia. I'm glad I caught you."

If London's attendance surprised her, Mia didn't show. Her poker face was better. "London. I didn't expect to see you here."

London rushed forward and hugged her, even

though she knew Mia wouldn't like it. "I want to introduce you to Ezra." Turning to him, she said, "Ezra, this is my friend Mia. She's a curator at the Art Institute and she put me in contact with some gallery owners who might want me to do a show of my own."

"Nice to meet you, Ezra." Mia extended a hand.

Ezra's wide palm engulfed hers. "Nice to meet you, too."

"Ezra is an artist, too," London said. "He works in glass."

"Interesting. Have you seen anyone else we might know?"

London smiled, realizing that Mia was a little worried that the heist was happening tonight. "Well, Audrey and Jared are supposed to be here. Didn't they tell you?"

"He might've mentioned it, but I haven't seen them."

"Nikki is busy tonight. I asked her if she wanted to join us and she said it wasn't her kind of party."

"Whose kind of party?" Logan asked as he joined them and handed Mia a glass of champagne.

"Nothing," Mia said, accepting the glass and kissing his cheek. "London just introduced me to her date."

"Ezra, this is Logan, Mia's boyfriend. Logan, it's nice to see you again."

"Mia didn't mention that you were coming tonight."

"She didn't know. It was a last-minute decision because I wasn't sure if Ezra would be free."

Logan stood next to Ezra. "This isn't exactly my kind of party."

"Mine either," Ezra responded.

"Luckily, Mia doesn't drag me to these things too often."

"We can go after this drink. I just need to make the rounds, show my face. Let the world know that I've fallen in love. You know the drill."

The look Mia gave Logan melted London. Mia had always been a little cold and distant, but falling for Logan had changed her demeanor. "You two look so happy."

"We are," Mia said. "Let's go make those rounds now, so we can get out of here." She reached for Logan's hand. "We'll talk later," she said to London.

When they were gone, Ezra asked, "Is she really a friend? Or someone else you plan to steal from?

"Mia? She's a friend." As she spoke the words, London realized that she meant them. Mia was a real friend. London stepped closer and tip-toed up to whisper in his ear. "While she's no longer working with us, she set this entire plan in motion. Her full name is Mia Benson."

He looked down at her with wide eyes.

"I read that she played a role in her father's arrest."

"Yep." She hooked her arm into his again. "Like I said, not everyone here is bad."

They made their way around the room and

London led him into another room where a small band was playing music. "Let's dance," she said.

"I don't dance. Definitely not in a penguin suit."

"Just stand there and hold me." She reached up and wrapped her arms around his neck.

"That, I can do."

They swayed to the music. It was probably supposed to be some waltz or something like that, but London swayed with him like she was at a high school dance. She felt safe in his arms and allowed the rest of the world to disappear.

"I could get used to this," she said quietly.

He grunted a response, but it wasn't necessarily a bad grunt. It was just Ezra being Ezra.

"So this thing you do, how long are you going to keep doing it?"

"Not sure. Until we've run out of people to help."

"That could be forever. There's always someone in need."

"True, but we're working with a specific, distinct subset of people."

"Just that list of people? No one else?"

She paused. She'd never considered that they could expand what they do. "I never thought about it. I don't think my friends have either."

They danced until the end of the song, but when she moved to step back, he held her close. She didn't say anything, just waited for him to say what he needed.

"I understand why you do what you do."

That was a relief, but she heard a giant *but* coming.

"I don't know if I can sign on to be part of that. I've never done anything like that. Illegal."

Her heart sank a little. "I'm not asking you to participate."

"Even if I'm not an active participant, knowing makes me guilty, right?"

"I guess. If I were planning a murder, you might get into trouble for not reporting me. But this is white collar, money crimes."

"How am I supposed to sit by and wait for a phone call saying that you've been arrested? How can I build a relationship with you knowing that is a possibility?"

So many emotions crashed through her. She didn't have an answer for that. She'd never had that kind of worry over someone. "I think it would boil down to you trusting that we know what we're doing and we won't get caught. We don't take unnecessary risks."

"But it's still risky."

"More for my friends than me."

"But they could drag you down."

"They wouldn't."

"People do all kinds of things when they get desperate."

She stepped away from him and held his hand. "Let's move over here." She led him back toward the wall, away from tables, and dancers. He leaned one big shoulder against the wall and waited.

"Not long ago, Mia was put in a precarious situation. Her boyfriend, Logan, is an FBI agent. She was willing to give herself up to save us. The thing is, no one had anything on her. Her hands were clean."

"Then why would she take the fall? Obviously, it worked out for her."

"She was willing to confess because she cares about us. The same reason my friend Audrey sent you that package of information. We're more than a team. We're family."

"How many people have you helped?"

"Hundreds. We can't solve all the problems, but we can ease the pressure. Give them some breathing room."

"And they don't know who you are or where the money comes from?"

"Nope. All anonymous."

A slow smile spread on his face. "Then I guess that makes you better than Robin Hood. Everyone knew who he was."

"Does that mean you're willing to give us a shot?"

"I think so."

She squealed and jumped up to hug him, wrapping her arms tightly around his neck.

"One condition."

"Anything."

"No lies. I'd rather have the hard truth than soft lies because you think you're protecting me."

She remembered her conversation with Nikki about trying to protect those they love and the futile nature of it. "I can do that."

"Good. Then let's get the hell out of here. I can barely breathe in this thing."

As they headed out into the chilly night air, hand in hand, London couldn't help but think about the magic of Christmas. And Ezra's questions about continuing and helping more people fired ideas in her brain.

Maybe they could do more...

TO KEEP UP TO DATE WITH ALL OF SLOANE'S releases and get exclusive sneak peeks, sign up for my newsletter: https://www.subscribepage.com/sloanesteele

IF YOU HAVEN'T READ THE REST OF THE Counterfeit Capers series, read on for an excerpt from book 1 - *It Takes a Thief*

It Takes a Thief

EXCERPT

December

Jared waved at the doorman as he made his way to the elevator. He spent enough time here that no one expected him to sign in. When Mia first moved in, they stopped him every time, worried that he was an overbearing lover. The thought still made him cringe. Explaining that they were cousins gave him a pass to go up to her apartment without question.

When the door swung open, Mia looked surprised to see him. "What are you doing here?"

"Happy birthday." He bent and kissed her cheek. "Did you think I would let you spend your thirtieth alone?"

"Who says I plan to be alone?"

He glanced around the empty room, taking note of the open bottle of wine on the table and single glass beside it, and raised an eyebrow. The woman had lived barely above hermit status for years. She worked, spent time with her mother, and came home to a tastefully and artfully decorated condo. Alone. She'd been gun-shy ever since her engagement ended in a very public humiliation. Her face was free of makeup and she had her thick black hair tied back. She wouldn't let a new man see her bedtime routine, even though she still looked regal. Mia was like her mother in that way.

She huffed. "Fine. So I'm alone. I have things to do. Plans to make."

He took off his coat and hung it on the rack. Then he turned and handed Mia a wrapped gift.

"You know you didn't have to get me anything."

"Until you find some guy that will spoil you, I reserve the right. Everyone should have a gift on their birthday."

She tugged at the ribbon and slid her finger under the tape.

"Hey, you know you don't have to save the paper, right?"

"Leave me alone."

It was the same exchange they had every year, at her birthday and at Christmas. Mia was meticulous in her approach to everything. Jared preferred to dive in.

Moments later, she held up the thin diamond bracelet. "It's beautiful. Thank you."

She placed it back in the box and went to the liquor cabinet. After she handed him a glass, they settled on the couch in front of the marble fireplace where a fire burned.

He picked up the open bottle and poured

himself some white wine. "Are you slumming to-day? Since when you do you drink regular wine? No vintage Dom for your birthday?"

"There is nothing regular about Domaine Leflaive, thank you very much."

"So what has you so busy you're not cele-brating with a party?"

She sniffed. "As if. That's the last thing I would do."

He set his glass on the table without drinking any. "I thought things had gotten better for you. You've been making the society circuit again."

Their fathers' crimes had taken a toll on Mia and he wished he could do something to repair the damage done. Both her mother and his felt like pariahs in the society they'd been a part of long be-fore they'd gotten married. In his personal life, he hadn't taken a hit, mostly because he was a man. Pro-fessionally, however, his dreams had been crushed.

"I've been to functions and other than the oc-casional whisper by the same catty trolls I've dealt with my whole life, it has been better. But no big celebrations with me in the spotlight."

"Other than sitting around in your pajamas and drinking alone, what are you doing?" He picked up his glass and drank the wine, even though he'd prefer whiskey.

She reached across the table and flipped open a file folder. He knew immediately what it was. The faces of men they'd grown up around, men who were their fathers' confidants and friends. "You're really doing this?"

Years ago Mia had come to him with a plan to

get back at the men who'd gotten rich with their fathers by bilking innocent people out of their life savings. She couldn't go after her own father or his because they'd fled the country. But she wanted to do something proactive.

"Did you think I was kidding? You should know better."

"I do. Part of me hoped it was a whim you'd plan out and never act on."

She laughed. "I would never waste my time. And now that I'm thirty, I have the funds to put everything in play."

Their mothers were smart women. They'd made their husbands sign prenups, which protected the Washington family fortune. Mia's and Jared's inheritances were safe from the federal government. Their mothers also made sure the money wouldn't be wasted on immature whims, so they had to wait until their thirtieth birthdays to access the money.

"Let me help."

"It's dangerous. If I get caught, I don't want you going down with me."

That had always been her argument every time they discussed this. "Then we won't get caught. Wait until my birthday. I'll be able to foot half the bill for the plan."

"I've already waited five years."

"Then six more months won't matter." He was well aware of how long it had been. He'd just graduated law school and all of his plans and dreams had been sucked into the black hole of his father's dirty deeds. Who the hell would hire the spawn of a criminal? "It'll give us time to find the right people to carry this out."

She sipped her wine and studied him. His offer intrigued her, but Mia was not someone who liked to give up control.

"I can be very useful. I have connections you'll need and have no idea how to get." Once his law career had gone down the drain, he'd taken all the tools his father had instilled in him, and he'd learned to play in all the gray areas of the world. And he was damn good at it.

He'd embraced their fathers' teachings about business and people. While Mia had bucked against the lessons in manipulation, he'd made a career from it.

"I don't want to use people who know us, who we are. Word will spread and our anonymity will be lost."

"*You* should know better," he said, throwing her own words back at her. "The players I know on the dark web never reveal their identities. It's a given that we all use aliases."

She sipped more wine. "All right, then. Let's talk about who we'll need. A thief, obviously."

"A hacker, someone who can get past security systems." Immediately he thought of Data. He'd used her services many times over the last few years. Efficient and relatively cheap. "I have someone I can reach out to when the time is right."

Mia crossed the room and returned with a small notebook and pen. She made a few notes. "I've been looking for a forger, but I haven't found anyone I like."

It figured she would start with the forger. Art was her area of comfort.

He chuckled. "You don't have to like them."

"I'm aware. I meant I don't like the quality of their work in conjunction with their attitudes. It's as if making a forgery isn't enough. They want to make it *better*."

"I'll put some feelers out for a thief while you continue to hunt for a forger." He leaned back on the couch and drank the rest of his wine.

She paused in taking notes, tapping her pen on the pad. "What about selling the artwork once we have it?"

"I can definitely find buyers."

Her jaw muscle pulsed. It was a small twitch, but he knew his cousin. He leaned forward, resting his elbows on his knees. "Is there a problem?"

"It suddenly feels like you're taking over. I've spent years gathering information and planning this, and now you walk in and want to handle all of the active pieces."

He sighed and shook his head slightly. "We each have a skill set. You've utilized yours master-minding this plan. Let me use mine to help you carry it out."

She didn't seem convinced. He reached over and laid a hand over hers. "This is my legacy, too."

Sometimes it seemed like she forgot he shared the same guilt she felt.

"Fine. But I make all final decisions. This is what I have so far." Spreading the images from the folder across the coffee table, she ticked off the list of twelve—men who not only aided and abetted their fathers, but who also got rich off the same scheme.

"How do you see this working?" he asked.

"I'm still developing the list of artwork they have. We'll only get one shot, so I want to choose the piece from each of them that will hurt. I'll commission a forgery. Then the thief goes in, swaps the forgery for the original and we sell the original."

"And then?"

"We use the money to make some reparations for what they did. We might not be able to repay every family, but we can make a difference."

He smiled. That was the cousin he knew—all cold steel on the outside but a soft, mushy center. "And how do you decide who gets the money?"

"I haven't figured that piece out yet. I have a list of names, people who came forward and publicly criticized our fathers for what they did. That is one way you can help. They can't know it's coming from us and you can dig around and see who needs the most help. Prioritize who needs what."

Jared nodded and considered who he could have do background checks on the victims. He picked up Mia's notebook and saw a list on the inside cover. It took a minute, but he recognized the lessons. Their fathers had said these mantras as if they were motivational quotes:

Spending money to get the best is worth it 99% of the time.

Endearing yourself to others makes it easier to manipulate them.

Loyalty to the right people is vital to success.

He'd assumed that Mia had never paid attention to the rules for business. She'd been an art history major, after all. She preferred the pretty things in life over the gritty side of making money.

He pointed at the list. "Why have this here?"

"Because I plan to use their life lessons against them." She splayed her hands across the photos. "I'm going to teach all of them—including our fathers—Mama's lesson: actions carry consequences."

Karma might be a bitch, but it had nothing on Mia. This summer was going to be interesting.

***

Green: I know it's the holidays, but are you available?

Data: I'm always available for you.

As soon as she hit send, she cringed.

Green: Interesting. I hadn't realized we'd arrived at that point in our relationship.

Data: I'm available for WORK. You know what I meant.

Green: Hmm… I think it might've been a Freudian slip.

Data: And I think your ego is too big. What kind of job?

Green: I'll send you photos. I need you to dig up some dirt.

Data: Oooo… Blackmail. Intriguing.

Green: I said nothing about blackmail.

Data: It was in the subtext. I read between the lines.

Green: It's all right for you to read between the lines but I'm not allowed?

Data: Glad we're clear. :)

She waited for the link to pop up and scanned the information he sent.

Data: What's your timeline?

Green: Soon. But given the holidays, I can wait the week.

Data: Got it. I'll let you know when I have info.

Audrey closed her laptop with a smile. Things usually quieted down for her over the holidays. She was grateful to have anything pop up, and the fact that Mr. Green had a job was all the better. The man always paid well, and at this point, she needed every penny she could get. After shoving her computer in her bag, she bundled up against the cold for her walk to the bus stop.

Before leaving the apartment, she glanced at her bedroom door. She'd been living here with Misty for almost three months, but over the last couple of weeks, she'd had the feeling that her room wasn't secure. Misty said she hadn't stepped foot in the room since Audrey moved in, but her roommate often had guests. The sleazy kind she brought home from her job at the strip club.

Her equipment was all she had of value and most of Misty's "dates" wouldn't have a clue what to do with any of it; she just didn't want creepy guys touching her stuff, so until she came up with a better lock, she carried her laptop with her. She patted her pocket to double-check that her present for Gram was still there. This was their first Christmas apart. Not really apart, but not living together. Three months ago she'd made the painful decision to sell everything she had and pour every penny into getting Gram the care she needed.

Audrey couldn't take care of her anymore.

The assisted living facility cost more than Audrey made, but Gram deserved the best care possible. So here she was on Christmas Eve trekking on the bus in twenty-degree weather to share Christmas with Gram. The dark sky made it feel closer to midnight than dinnertime.

Horizons looked like any other residence on the outside. Kind of stately but bland. Inside, they at least put in some effort to be festive. They had a Christmas tree in the corner of the lobby as well as a menorah on the reception desk. Audrey signed in without chatting with the receptionist and went straight to Gram's room.

Room. That was funny. Gram actually had more of an apartment than she did. Gram's place had a small kitchen as well as a living room—bedroom combo. Gram answered the door.

"Audrey? What are you doing here?"

"Hi, Gram. How are you? I thought we'd spend Christmas Eve together like we do every year."

"I don't know that I'm done being mad at you for sticking me here," Gram said as she walked away from the door.

Audrey took it as an invitation. She unwrapped her scarf and laid her jacket and bag on a side table near the door. Pulling the gift out, she said, "I brought you a gift."

"Pfft. Hope you weren't counting on anything. I'm like a prisoner here. I couldn't go shopping." She settled in her recliner facing the TV.

"They told me they do trips to the mall." In all likelihood, Gram had probably forgotten. That had been happening more and more. "Here."

She accepted the small package and peeled at the paper. It wasn't much, but Audrey had chosen a box of Gram's favorite chocolates, ones Gram typically only indulged in for special occasions. The doctor had said that small reminders might help prompt her memory.

"What's this?" She studied the box for a minute and then practically threw it at the table beside her. "I hate chocolate. Makes me sick."

"No, it doesn't, Gram. Remember? These are the ones filled with booze. They're your favorite."

She sniffed, a look of irritation on her face. "I never drink."

Audrey sighed and sat on the edge of the loveseat. So much for holidays with family. They fell into silence, except for the blaring of the TV showing reruns of *General Hospital*. Audrey longed to talk with Gram like they used to do.

Gram suddenly turned and looked at her. "Tina? What the hell are you doing here? I told you to stay away."

"Gram, it's me, Audrey."

Gram rose and jabbed a finger at her. "Don't you lie to me. Get out!"

Audrey's throat closed. This was why she'd been forced to bring Gram here. There had been more days of confusion than reality. Audrey missed Gram.

"Have a good Christmas," she said quietly as she picked up her jacket and bag and left.

On the bus ride back home, she swallowed tears. She'd believed she'd have more time with Gram. Being alone had never really bothered Audrey, but losing Gram was unfathomable.

She let herself into the apartment and stepped over three pairs of sky-high heels that Misty typically tossed when she walked through the door. A smudged mirror sat on the coffee table, alerting her to the fact that partying had been happening in her absence. Misty must've celebrated the holiday before going in to work.

She went straight to her bedroom. Burying herself in work was just the antidote for her abysmal thoughts. Mr. Green had given her a job, so that was where she would focus her energy. Spending the night digging into someone else's misery made her feel better about her own circumstances.

It didn't take long at all. Seven hours later, she had a dossier of dirt for her client. With it being almost three in the morning, she debated whether she should send it now or wait. It was officially Christmas, so would it be rude to interrupt his holiday? No, he was the kind of guy who worked around the clock. She didn't know how she knew that, but she did.

Data: I have a Christmas present for you.

She immediately rethought the message because the dude might not even be Christian. If he was Jewish would he be offended that she'd made the assumption? She sent the link to the file and set her laptop on the bed next to her with the intention of logging off for the night. But a message immediately bleeped at her.

Green: You work fast. I appreciate that.

Data: Don't you sleep?

Green: Of course. Do you?

Data: Sometimes

Green: Alone?

Audrey snickered. Where the hell did this guy get off asking if she slept alone?

Data: Sometimes. You?

Green: Sleeping? Always.

Hmm... Mr. Green was letting her know he was a player. She shouldn't care, but this was the most personal they'd ever gotten.

Data: Kind of a sad comment on your life. Not only do you always sleep alone but you're working on Christmas Eve.

Green: The same can be said of you.

Data: I'm just fulfilling the stereotypical image of a hacker sitting alone in a dark room playing with my gadgets.

Green: Oh, to be one of those gadgets.

She burst out laughing and she couldn't stop.

Misty suddenly pounded on her door but didn't wait for a response before swinging it open. "Are you okay?"

Audrey gulped air and swiped at the tears on her cheeks. "I'm fine."

"Damn, girl. You're always so quiet that when I heard the noise, I thought you were having a seizure." Misty placed a hand over her heart as if to calm it. She must've just gotten home from work. Although the baby pink hoodie and sweatpants might appear to be workout clothes, Audrey knew that was Misty's to-and-from-work outfit.

"I'm fine. Just laughing over something that probably shouldn't even be that funny."

"Okay." She turned, her overly teased and sprayed red hair looking like a cloud around her head.

"Thanks for checking on me." *It's good to know that if I die in this crappy room someone would notice.* Her computer bleeped again.

Green: I'm sorry. Did I offend you?

Data: Not at all. I was laughing so hard my roommate felt the need to check on me.

Green: That's good then. Have an excellent evening.

Data: It's closer to morning.

Green: Not for people like us.

A few minutes later, she received notification of payment. If Mr. Green kept her busy like this, paying for Gram's care wouldn't be too bad. She opened the payment email. Mr. Green included a note in the memo.

Get yourself a nice new gadget and think of me.

While there was no new gadget in her budget, thoughts of him would be hard to ignore.

Also by Sloane Steele

Writing as Sloane Steele

The Counterfeit Capers

It Takes a Thief

Between Two Thieves

To Catch a Thief

Counterfeit Capers Adult Coloring Book

Writing as Shannyn Schroeder

The O'Leary Family

More Than This

A Good Time

Something to Prove

Catch Your Breath

Just a Taste

Hold Me Close

The O'Malley Family

Under Your Skin

In Your Arms

Through Your Eyes

From Your Heart

The Doyle Family

In Too Deep

In Fine Form

Daring Divorcees Series

One Night with a Millionaire

My Best Friend's Ex

My Forever Plus-One

Stand Alones

Between Love and Loyalty

Meeting His Match

Hot & Nerdy Novellas

Her Best Shot

Her Perfect Game

Her Winning Formula

His Work of Art

His New Jam

His Dream Role

About the Author

Sloane Steele is the pen name for Shannyn Schroeder. Shannyn is a part-time English teacher, part-time curriculum editor, and full-time mom, even though her kids are pretty self-sufficient teens. In her downtime, she bakes cookies, reads romance, and watches far too much TV.

If you want to connect with Sloane (and Shannyn):

www.SloaneSteele.com

Sign up for her newsletter here: https://www.subscribepage.com/sloanesteele

https://twitter.com/SSchroeder_

https://www.facebook.com/shannyn.schroeder/

https://www.instagram.com/sloanesteeleauthor/

About the Author

Sloane Steele is the pen name for Shannyn Schroeder. Shannyn is a part-time English teacher, part-time curriculum editor, and full-time mom, even though her kids are pretty self-sufficient teens. In her downtime, she bakes cookies, reads romance, and watches far too much TV.

If you want to connect with Sloane (and Shannyn):

www.SloaneSteele.com

Sign up for her newsletter here: https://www.subscribepage.com/sloanesteele

https://twitter.com/SSchroeder_

https://www.facebook.com/shannyn.schroeder/

https://www.instagram.com/sloanesteeleauthor/

www.ingramcontent.com/pod-product-compliance
Lightning Source LLC
Chambersburg PA
CBHW010845190726